CORNELIUS

Tanya R. Taylor

**~ Readers' Favorite Silver Medal Award Winner,
Number one bestseller and first book in
THE CORNELIUS SAGA SERIES ~**

About The Author

Tanya R. Taylor is a Readers' Favorite International Award-winning Author and has wowed readers with her riveting plots and compelling themes.

She is the author of several #1 bestsellers on Amazon and published her first book titled: 'A Killing Rage' as a young adult. Having worked in the financial arena, she is also a seasoned ghostwriter. Her book 'Cornelius' climbed to #1 in the Teen & Young-adult Multi-generational Family Fiction category on Amazon and is The Readers' Favorite

Silver Medal Award Winner in the Teen & Young-adult Paranormal genre. Her Supernatural, Suspense/Thrillers - 'CARA' and 'INFESTATION: A Small Town Nightmare' are multiple times #1 international bestsellers.

Tanya writes in various genres including: Paranormal Romance, Fantasy, Thrillers, Science-fiction, Mystery and Suspense.

TABLE OF CONTENTS

ACKNOWLEDGEMENTS

I dedicate this book to my former high school English & Literature teacher — Mrs. Shona M. Knowles. Mrs. Knowles recognized in me what I didn't quite see in myself at the time. She saw raw, creative talent and encouraged me to utilize my writing skills. Now, because of her encouragement and selfless contribution, I am able to put the word 'Author' next to my name and thus, make my loved ones proud. I am also grateful for the fact that my work and name will continue to live on long after I have passed on.

So, because of this, I dedicate **'Cornelius'** to this lovely lady who is well-deserving of so much more. If you ever ask her, she'll tell you that the name—Cornelius—has sentimental meaning to her.

A *special thank you* to my husband, my children, my parents and friends. Daddy, you always said to "Think Big" and instilled in me the confidence I needed to achieve great things. I truly appreciate that.

I would also like to thank everyone else who supported me and continues to support me in all of my endeavors.

I love you all.

PROLOGUE

It was a day and age much like today where every town, generation and household held firmly its secrets—torrid improprieties they would protect to the end of the world. Yet some secrets back then were far too shocking and disturbing to contain—ones entangled with emotions of such intensity that would shock the very life out of 'innocent', reserved folk.

The year was 1861. The town of Mizpah was on the verge of the abolition of slavery. White people with a conscience and black folk alike prayed and fought long and hard for the day when all human beings were considered equal in the eyes of the law.

Cornelius Ferguson, only the wealthiest planter in all of Mizpah, didn't support the views of the abolitionist movement in that territory nor in any other for that matter. Negro labor was highly favorable for his pockets and he couldn't imagine conducting his plantation affairs by any other means.

June 12th of 1861 was the day his life would forever change. It was the day a colored girl by the name of Karlen Key walked through his door. She was beautiful, literate, well-spoken — a rare breed and long- awaited trade off from another planter across the river. Cornelius had been anticipating her arrival. Germina, a rotund, elderly house slave with a few long strands protruding from her chin, met Karlen at the door and showed her where to put her tattered bag. Cornelius stood thirty feet away in the great room facing the entrance way, highly pleased and mesmerized by the new addition to his household. Karlen's eyes met his for a brief moment before she quickly lowered her head, made a slight bow and greeted her master. The twenty- one-year-old had no idea that her arrival at the Ferguson plantation would alter the course of her life and those around her in a most uncanny way.

1

Summer of 1965

"Wade! Mira!" Sara Cullen called her kids from outside the kitchen door. "Time to come inside and get yourselves cleaned up for dinner!"

Fourteen-year-old, Wade and thirteen-year-old, Mira were in the road playing 'bat and ball' in front of their yard with Monique Constantakis and her cousin Philip. Mira had just swung the bat for her turn to run the bases.

"Let's go!" Wade shouted to his sister as she considered one last run before heading inside. "If you don't come now, I'm leaving you and you'll be in big trouble with Dad." On that, he took off up to the driveway of their home and Mira, with a tinge of disappointment, handed the bedraggled, semi-splintered bat to Monique who was standing behind her.

"See you later," Monique said, visibly disappointed that her new friend had to leave.

"Yeah," Mira said before heading up the driveway behind her brother who had disappeared into the house.

The table, as usual, had been beautifully set for dinner. Sara Cullen was a true perfectionist and wanted everything to be just right when her husband of fifteen years, Michael, stepped into the dining room for his meal. She worshipped the dirt the man walked on and kept herself in the finest physical shape she could possibly manage. She was five feet, ten inches tall, and remarkably thin. Her hair was long, black and curly, and her features narrow. Michael Cullen was not the most attractive man in the world, but he carried big, broad shoulders and a six-pack most men would die for. Furthermore, he collected a handsome paycheck at the end of each week, lived in a nice neighborhood, and sported a two-year-old red Jaguar. Nevertheless, Sara—Head Nurse at Freedom Hospital— could not be accused of being with him solely for his money or his executive status at the State-run Gaming Board. They had met fresh out of high school when all they had ahead of them were nothing more than dreams and aspirations.

Mira sat at the table first though Wade had been the first to wash up.

"Wade! Where are you?!" Sara cried, as she hurried around placing the remaining items on the table. The boy showed up moments later.

"Where were you all that time?" Sara asked. "You know I like both of you to be seated before I call your dad out."

"I had to... brush my hair." Wade lowered his head slightly.

"That's a lie!" Mira blurted with a wide smile. "He had to use the toilet!"

"Liar!" Wade rebutted.

"You had to use the toilet! You had to use the toilet!" Mira sang.

"Now stop it - both of you!" Sara barked. "This is no time for games... and wipe that smile off your face Mira; I'm not playing!"

"Yes, Mother," Mira softly replied.

The children composed themselves and waited patiently for their father who emerged a few minutes later from the master bedroom.

"Kids..." Michael hailed straight-faced as he sat down.

Both children responded monotonically, "Hi, Dad."

Sara joined them moments later.

As was customary for the family, they all bowed their heads at the sound of Michael's utterance, "Let us pray" before diving into their meals.

From her chair, Mira watched as her mother talked and talked to her father while he engaged very little in the conversation. It was like that all the time and Mira was beginning to wonder why her mother even tried. What Sara saw in Michael that was so appealing and attractive totally eluded Mira. Michael was a brutally rigid man who, in his daughter's opinion, always seemed to wish he was somewhere else other than at home.

"May I be excused?" Mira asked fifteen minutes later, wanting to escape the drab, depressive atmosphere of the room.

"But you hardly touched your casserole," Sara said, noticing for the first time that her daughter had barely eaten.

"I'm not hungry."

"Are you all right, honey?" Sara asked, as Michael continued his meal supposedly unaffected.

"Yes, Mom. I just feel a bit tired and would like to lie down," Mira replied.

"You may leave," Michael said, not making eye contact.

"Well then…" Sara continued, "I'll cover your plate for you in case you get hungry before bedtime."

"Thanks Mom." Mira backed out from the table and retreated to her bedroom.

Approximately a half hour later, there was a light tap at the bedroom door. The doorknob turned slowly, then

Sara walked in. "Are you all right?" She asked Mira who was curled up in bed with a Sherlock Holmes mystery.

"Sure." Mira sat up as her mother proceeded to the side of the bed.

She felt her daughter's forehead with the back of her hand. "No fever. That's good. Are you sure you're okay?" The look she gave was a combination of suspicion and concern.

"Yes. I'm really fine, Mom. I just wasn't hungry; that's all—I guess from all that running around earlier."

"I see." Sara got up. "Well, like I said… if you get hungry later, your food is right there covered in the refrigerator. Wouldn't want you going to bed empty only to wake up all gassy in the morning."

Mira smiled. Her mother reached down and kissed her on the forehead. "I love you, sweet pea."

"I love you too, Mom."

2

"You wanna go by the canal today?" Wade asked Mira at the kitchen counter. An early riser, he had been up for well over an hour, but she had just gotten out of bed.

"Dad said we can't go back there—you know that," Mira answered, cracking an egg over a bowl.

"He's not here. Mom's not here. They don't have to know," Wade replied. "We can get our fishing rods, some bait, and maybe this time, we'll actually catch something."

"I don't know… the last time we got caught out there we almost got a good whipping. Dad's hand was itching. Luckily, he let us off the hook with a warning. Off the hook… got it?"

"Look! They're both at work. We'll only be gone for a few hours and will be back long before they get here. They'll never know, so we're not risking anything." Wade was adamant.

"I don't know, Wade," Mira said, pouring a little cream into the bowl with her egg.

"Why are you so scared?" Wade asked. "We've been to the canal dozens of times and only got caught that one time when dad pulled up out of nowhere. You think he's gonna drive all the way home from work today on a sneaky suspicion that we're at the canal again and bust us for not listening? Come on, Mira!"

"Okay, okay. We can go after I've had my breakfast. I suppose you've eaten already?" Mira asked.

"Yeah. I'm cool. I'll go pack the gear."

The canal was less than a block away. It usually took the kids a mere four minute walk to get there. Mira, dressed in a yellow and white striped blouse and red shorts walked quickly behind her brother, inwardly hoping and praying that their father would not pull up and surprise them while they were on the way to the 'forbidden place'.

"We need to walk faster," Mira said, now over-taking her brother. Wade silently caught up with her and in no time, they were at their favorite spot.

The canal was the only one in their neighborhood. It extended miles out to the sea. Several gated houses with boat decks surrounded it, except for a fifty-foot open area that was partially clear due to low, sparse bushes and a padded, gravel area kept in check by occasional vehicles driving through.

Mira sat down at the edge of the canal, her feet dangling against its rocky structure. Wade got the fishing rods ready before sitting next to her. He handed Mira a rod with bait attached and threw his out into the not-so-shallow water. For a while, they just sat there looking out into the water at tiny schools of fish swimming around.

"What's on your mind?" Wade asked, still looking straight ahead.

"What do you mean?" Mira glanced at him.

"You're so quiet. What're you thinking about?"

"Nothing."

"You're the one lying now," Wade said.

"How can you say that I'm lying? Are you inside my brain, Wade Cullen?" Mira returned feistily.

"It's Mom and Dad, isn't it?"

Mira looked at him. "How do you know?"

"I know what's been going on. I can see it was getting to you. That's why you left the table yesterday, right?"

For a few moments, there was silence, then Mira finally answered: "I don't understand why Mom tries so hard to please Dad. It's not like he shows her he appreciates anything she does anyway."

"We've never known Dad to be a talkative person, Mira. He doesn't say much to us neither," Wade replied.

Again… there were a few moments of silence.

"I think his actions go beyond not being much of a talker, Wade. Dad can be so cold at times. I feel so bad for Mom when I see her trying so hard to please him all the time and he doesn't seem to be giving anything back to her. It's like she's in a relationship all by herself."

17

"Mom's used to Dad. They're just different people. She doesn't seem to mind when she's talking to him and it's obvious that he's not even listening. If she's not bothered by it, why should you let it bother you?"

"Because she's our mother, Wade. That's why. She deserves better than that," Mira answered.

"Better than Dad?"

"I think so."

Wade was shocked that his sister's feelings about the matter were that intense. "What are you trying to say, Mira—that Dad's not good enough for Mom? Don't you love him?"

"Sure I do. I love them both, but I can tell that Mom's not happy. She pretends that she is because she lives in this 'perfect world' that she's created in her head."

Wade's eyes were on the water again. "I think I feel something..." he said moments later. "Yes! I got a bite!" He reeled in the rod as quickly as he could while Mira's eyes beamed at the prospect of him making a good catch. By then, they were both standing and watching an average-sized snapper wiggle its streamlined body on the hook.

"Yay! We got one!" Mira exclaimed.

Wade unhooked the fish and dumped it into their mother's mini cooler.

"That's a good one," Mira said, watching the fish flop around in the cooler.

"Yeah. Let's see if we can catch anymore."

They both sat back down and re-tossed their fishing rods after Wade baited his again.

A half hour passed and there was nothing. Wade could now sense Mira's restlessness. "You wanna wait a little while longer to see if we'll get another bite?" He asked.

"Na. Let's not push our luck," Mira said. "We got a fish. Let's go fry it."

After turning onto their street, Mira's eyes hit the large property straight ahead at the end of the corner. "You wanna go see if any dillies are on the trees? We can eat them with our fish," she said excitedly.

"The Ferguson property?" Wade asked.

"Yeah."

Since they would have to go past their house in order to get there, Wade said, "Okay. Let me take the cooler inside first."

Mira waited in the western side of the yard that was adjacent to the road. She was so relieved that the canal trip went well and was eager to season and fry the fish they had caught.

"Let's go," Wade appeared a minute later with an empty, plastic bag balled up in his hand. "Wanna race there?"

"Sure. Now!" Mira took off on her brother unexpectedly and knowing he had been duped, Wade ran with all his might to try and catch up to her. Mira had

19

almost made it first to the edge of the Ferguson property before Wade's long legs finally caught up to her and overtook her. He was going so fast that he could barely cut his speed sufficiently before nearly slamming into the huge coconut tree directly in front of him. Mira laughed as she panted to catch her breath.

"You cheater!" Wade said after slumping under the tree.

"Don't blame me if I almost beat you here," Mira replied. "You always boast about being able to run faster than I can."

"Are you serious?!" Wade was flabbergasted. "I *can* run faster than you! Didn't I prove it again just now—even though you cheated, you little pipsqueak?!"

Mira advanced onto the large acreage and looked up at the dillies hanging temptingly from the large, outstretched tree branches of one of many trees that clustered the property. The Ferguson estate was comprised of approximately sixty acres of land which took up most of the road east to west, extending northwardly to the edge of another neighborhood. Wade and Mira had not walked even a good two acres of the land since they were old enough to 'explore'.

"This one's packed. You wanna climb?" Mira asked her brother. Wade was the official tree-climber of the pair since Mira was terrified of heights.

Wade got up off the ground holding his back like a man far beyond his years. "Okay. You know the drill," he said, handing her the bag.

As Wade climbed the tree, Mira readied the bag so that he could drop the dillies into it. In seconds, he was at arm's length from the nearest tree branch. It was laden with mostly semi-ripe dillies. "I'm gonna start dropping now!" He cried.

Mira opened the bag as widely as possible and positioned herself directly under her brother as he dropped the fruit one by one. As usual, the bag had missed a few of them and Mira was bending down picking up the ones that had fallen without bursting on impact.

"You can't run and you can't catch!" Wade laughed in the tree as he deliberately dropped some of the dillies while she was still stooping down to pick up the others.

"You're stupid for dropping them, Wade. You're really immature!" She snarled.

Deciding they had enough of them, Wade came down from the tree and snatched one of the dillies out of the bag. As he ate, he looked around at the large property and an idea struck him. "How about we explore this land? We've never gotten further than just a few feet in everytime we come here."

"This is private property, Wade. We can't just go exploring," Mira replied, thinking how *slow* her brother really was. After all, the large, lop-sided NO

TRESPASSING sign sprayed in red was clearly visible on the fence.

"You're gonna let an old NO TRESPASSING sign stop you from walking through here? Have you ever seen the owners out here? Have you ever seen *anyone* out here?"

Mira was quiet.

"Right! That's because no one ever comes here. The place is abandoned. What's wrong with a couple of kids just walking through a vacant property with a bunch of tall trees and bushes on it? What can we possibly do to hurt the land?" Wade said sarcastically. "Come on, Sis. It'll be fun. We can pretend that we're real explorers or something."

Mira was hesitant whenever Wade presented ideas that could possibly get them into trouble. Then again… those types of ideas were the only ones he ever seemed to come up with. "What about the fish?"

"What about it?" Wade was puzzled.

"We have to fry it before Dad and Mom get back home."

Wade looked at Mira in disbelief. "Why are you so darn scary, girl? How long do you think they've been gone? It's only been a few hours. Last I knew, they got off work in the evening and then there's traffic. It's barely noon yet."

"How do you know what time it is?" Mira asked. "You don't have a watch."

"I can estimate the time, Mira. Can't you, smarty pants?"

Mira shoved the bag of fruit at him. "Here then! You carry this." And she slowly headed out into the wooded area.

As they walked along a narrow trail, the children were fascinated by the size of the property. Trees of every kind imaginable seemed to inhabit it—pine, mangoes, bananas, avocadoes, plum, ginep. Wade and Mira stopped and picked what they wanted, adding them to the bag, and the apprehension Mira had initially felt about their so-called exploration had soon disappeared.

"This is great," she said, sucking on a plum.

"Awesome!" Wade agreed. "I feel like we're in the jungle or something. How long do you think it'll take us to walk the whole perimeter?"

Mira looked at him incredulously. "Are you out of your mind?" Do you think I'm gonna walk this entire property? I hear the Fergusons' land is more than a few miles long."

"I didn't mean we should walk the whole thing today. I was asking how long you think it would take us if we decided to," Wade explained.

"I don't know… maybe an hour or two." Then her eyes were suddenly affixed to a large house that they never knew was there. "Hey, look there!" Mira pointed straight ahead.

"Wow! That's huge!" Wade exclaimed, almost in slow motion. With heightened curiosity, he started running toward it.

"Wait up!" Mira shouted, careful to do so in a lowered voice as she had no idea who or what might be inside. "Don't go in there without me!"

However, old and dilapidated with broken windows showcased along the whole front view, the house was breathtaking.

Wade climbed the colonial-style porch, stopping just about a foot away from the front door. The only thing is… there was no door—just a ten foot opening where there, most likely, used to be double doors.

Wade looked inside. Grimy white tiles covered the entire front area as far as he could see.

Mira climbed the porch moments later. "Do you see anything?" She asked softly, feeling a bit of apprehension gradually returning.

"No," Wade whispered. "Is anyone in here?" He called out hoping not to receive an answer.

They stood quietly, both decidedly ready to take off in an instant if they heard even a crack. They waited for a few seconds… nothing. Then Wade said, in not so much of a whisper anymore, "Let's go in."

Mira grasped his arm. He was just eleven months older than she was, but in a case like that where they were entering the *unknown*, he could have very well been ten years older and fifty pounds heavier as she knew 'come hell or high water', he would protect her.

Before stepping inside, Wade looked at her, "You mind letting up a bit? You're squeezing my arm."

"Oh sorry," Mira replied nervously.

They walked inside together—eyes darting in all directions of the spacious interior. The white paint on the wall was chipped in several places and the dusty floor had been speckled with creature droppings and smudges of dirt and mud. There was no furniture in sight—just a large, empty space. Wade and Mira walked slowly ahead and entered a room that looked like an extension of the living room, only separated by an arched wall.

"Hello..." Wade called out again.

"Is anyone here?" Mira said behind him, voice breaking at the end.

They proceeded through the large front area then entered what looked like the kitchen. There was one row of cabinets still attached to the upper northern section of the wall with a few missing doors. Some doors were slanted due to rusty, broken hinges. There were three other sections of the wall where only the imprint of cabinets remained presenting a theory to the observer that they might have been cleanly extracted at some point by thieves.

"This place is a mess," Mira uttered, still holding her brother's arm.

"Yeah. You notice that just about every door around here is missing?"

"Yeah."

"Let's go upstairs," Wade released Mira's grip. "Follow me."

"No way! You know I'm afraid of heights!" Mira whispered loudly.

"Just hold on to the rail. You'll be fine," Wade replied before heading up the long winding staircase.

Feeling that she would rather be with him than downstairs alone in the old, creepy house that resembled something from a horror flick, she took a deep breath in and decided to follow him. The ceiling of the house was extremely tall and as Mira carefully followed Wade up the stairs, she couldn't help but wonder how the owners ever managed to change a light bulb up there whenever necessary. As they climbed the staircase, the wood beneath their feet creaked and Mira had no idea how she would ever get back down.

They made it to the second landing and refusing at that point to look down over the rail, Mira trailed closely behind Wade who had entered one of the bedrooms.

"Wow! This room is huge!" Wade remarked, hurrying over to a large window on the western side of the room. "Hee, hee!" He laughed looking down at the yard. "The second floor of this house must be at least a hundred feet from the ground!"

Mira quietly advanced toward the entrance of what looked like the walk-in closet. As she looked in, something immediately caught her eye. The floating image of a black woman was at the far end of the room. The apparition appeared relatively young with frazzled, black hair that hung tiredly just above her shoulders. Her face, rough and haggard, exuded a sadness that Mira could feel deep within her bones, and the thin, white dress the woman wore was drenched in what appeared to be blood around the mid-section where long trails of it had slid down to the end. Momentarily frozen by the sight of this woman, Mira's mouth hung open, yet no voice escaped. The woman's veiny eyes seemed to be begging, pleading...for something. Then her hand reached up toward Mira, re-enforcing what the little girl already felt was a cry for help. At that point, a blood-curdling scream escaped Mira's lungs and she darted outside of the room—Wade running behind her.

With a fear of heights that paled in comparison to what she saw in that room, before Mira knew it, she was at the bottom of the staircase and out of the house.

"What's wrong?" Wade called out to her in the yard. "Wait for me, Mira!"

She had run a good distance away from the house before even thinking of stopping.

"Tell me what's wrong!" Wade insisted after catching up to her. "I never saw you run that fast in my life."

"I know I shouldn't have listened to you, Wade. You're a jerk! We never should have come here," Mira blasted, walking hurriedly.

"What did *I* do?" Wade was confused.

"I don't wanna talk about it right now. I just wanna go home."

While darting out of the house, Wade had dropped the bag of fruits they had collected. The children walked home together without saying another word. Wade knew that he had to get to the bottom of what happened in that house; Mira was not going to fold up on him as she sometimes did. After all, he felt responsible for her and now guilty that she had been so traumatized by something that in spite of her fear of heights, she had run down a tall flight of stairs without giving it a second thought.

After arriving home, Mira went straight to her room and slammed the door. Wade went to the door and knocked lightly. "Mira… what happened back there?" He tried to turn the doorknob, but discovered it was locked. "Open up. I wanna talk to you."

"Go away!" Mira yelled.

With head hung low and feeling worse by the second, Wade asked: "What about the fish? Aren't we gonna fry it before Mom and Dad get back?"

"I don't care. Do what you want with it!" Mira replied.

"Why do you have to be like this? Why can't you just tell me what happened, Mira? You say I'm immature, but you're the immature one!"

Wade waited for a response, but didn't get one, so he went into the kitchen to prepare the fish. After scaling and seasoning their catch, he walked around to the side of the house, made an outdoor fire like he and Mira had done so many times and placed a tin frying pan on top of the heap. As the oil heated inside the pan, Wade sat on one of the two large rocks close by, elbow under chin, thinking of how good their day had been and how it ended up. He felt terrible for Mira and wished she didn't get in those quiet moods sometimes, thus closing herself off to the world. She didn't realize that whenever she did that, he felt completely lost.

After the oil came to a slight boil, he put the fish in the pan and watched as swarms of flies suddenly appeared out of nowhere around it. Shooing them away, Wade refused to go inside and cook on the stove: He and Mira had established something special together out there frying their catch on the make-shift stove, and no army of flies was going to change that.

After turning the fish over with a spatula, Wade looked up and saw Mira approaching. She went and sat down on the other large rock near the fire. Wade, elated that his sister had decided to join him, showed no reaction.

"The fish looks good," Mira said, looking at her brother.

Unable to hold back any longer, Wade asked: "What happened in that house, Mira? Why did you leave like that?"

29

Mira looked down for a moment. "I'm not sure. I thought… I saw something."

"Saw what?" Wade probed, curiosity in over-drive.

"I saw a woman, okay?" Mira decided to just get it out in spite of how crazy it might sound. "She was wearing a long, white dress—looked old fashioned to me—and it was covered in blood."

Wade gawked. "Are you serious?"

"'Course, I'm serious!" Mira snapped. "You think I would've took off like that for nothing?"

"Where was she?"

"In the closet."

"What was she doing?"

"Just standing there," Mira replied. "She seemed so sad. Well, I'm not going back there anymore. I don't care about dillies or anything else. I'm never going back on that property."

"I wonder why she's there." Wade was engrossed in thought.

"So you believe me?" Mira asked, feeling hopeful.

"Sure, I do. I know you'd never make something like that up. Besides, from the way you took off down those stairs, you had to see something." He laughed.

Mira smiled, then laughed out loud. Wade jumped on that opportunity to tease her as they sat and waited for their fish to cook.

3

The next day...

"Mister Cullen, could I get your signature, please?" Hollie Jefferson, the new executive secretary asked Michael on his way to the cafeteria. Hollie was twenty-five years old, had bleached-red, shoulder-length, curly hair and was stunning in appearance. Her bright, brown eyes had an intensity to them that most men found difficult to ignore.

"Sure, Hollie. What's this for?" Michael asked.

"Just a memo listing the minutes of the meeting this morning that the Board agreed we should circulate to the staff."

"I don't usually sign the memos. Are you sure you need me to sign this one?"

"Yes, sir. I have to get Mister Bridges' and Andy's as well," Hollie replied.

"Okay. No problem. You have to do what you have to do, right?" Michael smiled, fixing his stare a little longer than usual. Hollie smiled back as he pulled up a pen attached to his shirt pocket and signed the document.

"Thank you, sir," she said.

"You're welcome, Hollie." Michael started to leave, then glanced at his watch and said: "Ah... Hollie. I'm on my way to the caf to grab a cup of coffee. Would you like to join me?"

Hollie was surprised. As a young, newcomer to the Gaming Board, she never expected an older executive to show even the slightest bit of interest in her. She almost thought she would be invisible to the high-powered players since there were so many more established, well-educated, attractive women there. But then again, Hollie figured that her thoughts might be running way ahead of her: Maybe Michael's invitation to sit and have coffee was nothing more than a courtesy gesture for a newcomer. After all, he did wear his wedding ring every day.

"I would love to... Mister Cullen, but I have to get these memos sorted out," she replied.

"Come on..." Michael returned. "Those memos aren't going to run away. You have a fifteen minute coffee break at mid-morning. Use it."

She bit her lip for a second. "Okay, let's go then."

They took an elevator to the fourth floor and as they headed for a table, Michael went up ahead and pulled out a chair for Hollie.

"Thank you," she said, sitting down.

"I'll go and grab the coffee. Sugar and cream?" He asked.

"Yes. Two sugars please," Hollie replied appreciatively.

Michael returned minutes later with two cups of coffee in hand and carefully handed one to her. "So how are you liking it here?" He asked after sitting down and taking his first sip.

"I'm loving it so far," Hollie replied. "It's nice working with Mister Bridges."

"Dwight's cool. He's been at The Board for about thirty years or so. Did you know that?"

"No, sir. He didn't mention it." Hollie stirred her coffee.

"I met him here. He kind of showed me the ropes when I first arrived," Michael said.

"I see. So, how long have you been working here?"

"Only twenty-two years," Michael answered.

"Wow! I guess I've got a long way to go. My three months seem like nothing compared to the time you two put in."

"The years fly by quickly," Michael replied. "It feels like I've only just pulled up on the job yesterday for the first time. That's how fast time flies."

For a few moments, Michael and Hollie sat quietly sipping the coffee that had soon turned warm.

"So, are you married?" Michael asked, breaking the silence.

Just then, Hollie's feminine radar immediately went up. She was now convinced that her initial thoughts concerning Michael's invitation were, indeed, correct. Most, if not all men—in her opinion—who asked if she was married, were interested in being more than friends.

She cleared her throat. "Um… no." She held her head down, stirring the coffee again.

"What're you waiting for?" Michael asked with a cunning expression he could not hide.

"For the right time, I guess… and also, the right guy. Haven't come across Prince Charming as yet."

"An attractive girl like you should have men making fools out of themselves just to be with you. What're you doing to drive them away?"

"Nothing. Absolutely nothing. Men today aren't that serious about commitment. They don't know what they want, who they want or how they want it. All they know is they *want*," she replied rather boldly, noticing his gold wedding band again.

"Well, I agree with you to a certain extent. Many of us are just mixed up on the whole and then some of us know exactly what we want in life, but settle for what we have already without pursuing what we'd prefer. You know what I mean?" He commented.

"I think I do." Their eyes met and in that stare, there was no denial. Hollie knew why she was sitting at that table with Michael Cullen—a man with a powerfully confident demeanor and a physique that could make a woman's mind wander off in the wrong direction.

"Well, I think we'd better go now," she was looking at her watch. "It's 10:30. Wouldn't want to get in trouble with Mister Bridges."

They both got up together.

"Ah... don't worry about Dwight. He doesn't sweat the light stuff," Michael said.

"I know, but I'm still new on the job and I want to continue to give a good impression."

"I understand," Michael replied, and after entering the elevator together, he looked at her and asked: "So how about lunch sometime?"

"I... guess so," Hollie responded, figuring there was no harm having an innocent lunch with a fellow co-worker regardless of his intentions.

"Okay. Great!"

At the parting of the doors, they went in separate directions; Michael walking on with a smile and Hollie with uncertainty.

* * * *

"Why does this cooler smell like... fish?" Sara asked after opening the lid in the kitchen. She had just gotten home from work several minutes earlier and wanted to get dinner started before Michael arrived. It had been the same routine for years: She would knock off at 4:00 p.m. and hurry home so that dinner would be cooked by the time he arrived which was usually between 5:45 and 6:00 p.m. Sara was grateful to have always been on a fixed schedule at work for most of her marriage when many nurses she knew worked shifts. With Michael in mind, she took the job at Freedom Hospital ten years earlier making it clear that she could not work shifts and whenever they tried to force her, she would threaten to quit. Apart from taking to her, Gwen Dames, Sara's superior, considered her one of their most gifted nurses at the hospital and didn't want to run the risk of losing her.

"Fish?" Mira returned, glancing at Wade who was sitting next to her at the counter.

"Have you two been fishing lately?" Sara asked.

"Fishing? Didn't Dad tell us we couldn't go back to the canal?" Mira answered plainly.

Sara stood on the opposite side of the counter looking at her children suspiciously.

"Mom, are you sure you're smelling right?" Wade asked. "You had meat in that cooler that you took over to your friend's house just last week."

"Not fish... but I guess I might not have killed the scent properly while washing it. You sure you kids haven't been to that canal lately though? You know if your dad found out you did, you'd get a good butt whipping this time. It's really dangerous out there," Sara said with a hand on her side.

"We know, Mom," Mira replied. "We won't take a chance getting on Dad's wrong side."

While Sara took the cooler over to the sink to wash, Mira nudged Wade to follow her outside.

"Just going in the yard, Mom," Mira said on their way out.

"Okay, kids. Just come back soon to wash up for dinner."

"Okay, Mom," Wade replied.

"You idiot! You didn't wash out the cooler?" Mira charged as they walked around the side of the house.

"I gave it a little rinse. I didn't know she'd smell fish whenever she went to use it," Wade returned.

Mira shook her head hopelessly. She was beginning to really wonder if her brother had a functioning brain upstairs or if it happened to be positioned in the wrong place—short-circuiting whenever he sat down. "You know you should use bleach to kill the scent, Wade. I don't know what's wrong with you! You could've gotten us into trouble!"

"Well, you could have cleaned it, Einstein. I cleaned, seasoned and fried the fish without *your help* yesterday and you have the nerve to complain about me not washing the cooler too? You're just a selfish moron who like to whine all the time and not help out like you should. I'm going back inside. Stay out here by yourself!"

Wade stormed off and left Mira standing several feet away from where they had fried the fish. She was

37

suddenly feeling that, in a way, Wade might be right. She really wasn't much help the other day. He had done everything—even happened to catch the fish."

"Wade..." Mira called out to him just before he turned the bend towards the kitchen door, "...I'm sorry."

At dinner that evening, it was the usual routine between Mira and Wade's parents. Michael, detached as usual, focused on eating his meal—managing to get in a few 'uh huhs'—while Sara constantly talked. At one point, Mira rolled her eyes and shook her head in disgust.

"We're all done. The food was great, Mom. Can we go now?" Mira asked anxiously.

"You two can leave..." Michael responded evenly.

"You coming?" Mira looked at Wade.

He got up and they both retreated to Mira's room and closed the door behind them.

For a few moments, Sara tapped lightly on the table.

"Do you mind not doing that?" Michael asked sharply.

"Oh, I'm sorry. Didn't realize it was bothering you." She placed her elbow on the table and hand against her cheek. "Are we in trouble, Mike?"

The question startled her husband, but he continued to eat. "Trouble? What kind of trouble?"

"Marital trouble... relationship trouble," Sara replied.

"Why do you ask that?"

"I don't know," she sighed. "I guess I felt it for a long time, but just didn't bother to say anything. You seem so disconnected from all of us and for quite a while now. You weren't always like this Michael. You're not happy being with me anymore?"

Michael paused for a moment and looked at her. "For me, marriage isn't about being happy."

"It's not?" Sara was surprised by his answer.

"It's not." He wiped his mouth with a napkin. "It's about honoring the commitment I made to you by providing a good home for you and my children, a good education for them, and everything else you all would possibly need. As a man, I'd like to think I've done that."

"You *have* done that, honey... and still doing it. You're a wonderful husband and father and I would never want to be with anyone else."

"So, it's not about being happy," Michael continued. "It's about being responsible—about each of us doing our part to keep this family going in the right direction."

"Do you think I've been doing my part?" Sara asked, still madly in love with the man after so many years.

"I can't complain," Michael answered apathetically.

"I just think that we're not where we used to be as a couple, Mike. We used to sit and talk for hours and really plug in to each other. Now it's different. You barely speak to me and I keep trying so hard to reconnect with you, but it seems like nothing I'm doing is working."

"You talk enough for both of us," Michael cracked a smile.

"I'm not joking, Michael. Did you ever think that maybe the reason I talk so much is because I'm trying desperately to get you to engage in conversation with me?"

"You were always a talker, Sara. I met you like that. Besides, how do you expect me to *engage* if you're always running your mouth?!"

The sarcastic nature of his reply in the face of the out-pouring of her heart to him stung Sara like a bee. She got up, picked up their plates and went into the kitchen. Standing at the sink, she struggled to fight back the tears. A few, however, managed to escape down her chin as she still felt the coldness in Michael's words and the feeling that deep inside, he knew he was no longer in love with her. She listened as he backed out his chair, got up and walked toward their bedroom. Seconds later, she heard the door close and at that moment, she could no longer restrain the tears. She stood alone with an overwhelming sadness and a sense that she was slowly losing control of her life by no longer feeling or sensing Michael's love.

That night, after crawling into bed, Mira switched off the stubby, pink lamp on her nightstand. She and Wade had been watching television together for hours before she got sleepy and chased him out of her room. Their parents had retired to bed already and the house was quiet and still.

Lying in darkness as she started to drift off to sleep, Mira heard a loud whisper nearby: *"Have… you… seen… him?"*

Startled, she quickly reached over and switched on the lamp.

"Have… you… seen… him?" repeated the ghastly entity that was standing at the side of her bed.

Mira screamed at the top of her lungs and ran out of the room.

"Mom! Dad!" She barged into her parents' bedroom switching on the light. "Someone's in my room!"

"What?!" Michael got up quickly, retrieving the bat he had always kept next to his bed. "You two stay here."

Sara held Mira firmly as Michael left the room.

He carefully advanced towards Mira's bedroom. At the entrance, he felt for the light switch and flipped it on. Walking inside with his wooden weapon held ready to strike, Michael proceeded over to the closet area. Using the bat to sift through the clothing, he saw - no one. Bending down at the foot of the bed and looking under, he saw - nothing. He checked the window; it was locked. Immediately thinking of Wade, he hurried across the hallway to the boy's room, did a thorough check, and again, no one was anywhere in sight.

"What's wrong, Dad?" Wade asked sleepily.

"Nothing. Go back to sleep," Michael replied, switching off the light and closing the door behind him.

He went to check the remainder of the house, including the doors which he discovered were all still locked from the inside. By the time he headed back to his bedroom, Mira and Sara were waiting in the doorway.

"No one's out there," Michael said.

"But I saw a woman!" Mira insisted. "She was standing right next to my bed!"

"A woman?" Sara's expression was one of shock.

"Yes—a black woman wearing a long, white dress. It was all covered in blood. I saw her yesterday... at the Ferguson house."

"Where?" Michael asked.

"The Ferguson house. Wade and I went over there to pick dillies and we walked a little further up the trail and saw the house."

"You mean Cornelius's house?" Michael probed.

"Cornelius? Who's Cornelius?" Mira was puzzled.

"Come," Michael took her hand with a slight sense of urgency. They sat down together on the bed while Sara remained near the doorway.

"I don't want you or your brother going back to that house," Michael's expression left no doubt about the gravity of the matter.

"Okay," Mira answered sheepishly.

"Why not, Dad?" Wade walked inside the room rubbing his eyes.

"Because I said so!"

"Don't you think you should explain to them *why*?" Sara asked, moving in closer as Wade sat down on the bed.

Michael was silent for a few moments, then releasing a heavy sigh he said: "Cornelius Ferguson was the owner of that house. He passed away many, many years ago—long before your mother and I were even born." He glanced at Sara, then shifted back between the children. "It's been rumored that since his death, over the years several families lived inside that house and every one of them experienced something out of the ordinary that caused them to abruptly pack up and leave. They say that none of the families that moved in since Cornelius died remained there for more than just a couple of months. The house has now been vacant for many years because of all the stories; no one has since been brave enough to buy the place."

"Have you ever been there, Dad?" Wade asked curiously.

"One time ago, when your mom and I first moved into the neighborhood, after hearing the stories, I decided to take a little stroll through the property. I guess I'd say I walked a good distance in before I spotted the house due to the land being so large and overgrown with all those tall trees and bushes, but I never went inside."

"Why not?" Mira asked.

"I don't know." Michael shrugged. "I just didn't have a good feeling about it."

Wade and Mira were completely engrossed in the tale their father was sharing.

"So, that's why I don't want you two going anywhere near that house anymore," Michael continued.

"We can't pick anymore dillies and stuff?" Wade asked, disappointed. "The ones we get are right near the edge of the property."

Michael thought for a moment. "Okay... but don't go any further."

"Yes Dad," Wade replied.

"So, you're okay now, honey?" Sara asked Mira.

"I guess. But can I sleep in here with you tonight?" Mira was hopeful.

"You can sleep in my room," Wade said. "Let's go."

Mira got up, kissed her father and mother, then followed Wade to his room.

4

"How are we this morning, Mister Sherlong?" Sara Cullen asked cheerfully, as she entered the patient's private room.

"*We* are doing just fine, Freedom Queen," the sixty-five-year-old heart attack survivor affectionately responded. It was a nick-name he had pasted upon Sara the first time she walked in to check on him. Johnny Sherlong was a short man with a large, round belly. He stood at five feet, three inches tall, had balding white hair, an out-of-control moustache and prickly beard. He always wore a white, sleeveless shirt and couldn't seem to feel cold air no matter how cold the temperature got.

"I see you haven't eaten much of your breakfast," Sara said, eyeing the items on the gray tray next to his bed.

"I don't like hospital food. The taste'll kill ya before your heart does," Sherlong replied.

Sara started laughing, simultaneously checking his file she had brought with her. "You must eat, Mister

Sherlong. Think of it as fuel to keep up your strength. You do want to get better soon… don't you?"

"Yeah. You're right. How about you come a little closer so I can gather my strength?" He devilishly proposed.

"Oh, Mister Sherlong… Mrs. Sherlong needs to keep a tight leash on you." Sara tucked his pillow. "I bet no heart attack is going to keep you in line after you get out of here."

"How do you know so good, queen? This old stud ain't slowin' down for nobody. When I kick the bucket, I'm gonna go out punchin'… if you know what I mean," he winked.

Sara shook her head and picked up the tray. "I'm coming back to check on you later, okay?"

"Why can't you be my regular nurse?" Sherlong asked, rather peeved.

"Because Jennifer and the others are doing just fine taking care of your every need throughout the day. That's why."

"Not every need," the old man returned, slyly.

"You're right… just the ones that apply to why you're here," Sara said before leaving.

"Sherlong still cutting up with you?" Beverley started walking alongside Sara in the corridor.

"He wouldn't give it a rest," Sara replied.

"His wife's got a real player on her hands there. No wonder the guy had a heart attack; he's trying to keep up with all you young things."

Sara was a few months shy of forty and Beverley was twelve years older than she was. Beverley was tall, lanky, and always wore a shoulder-length, brown wig at work. The reason she gave Sara was that it was easier to throw on than trying to tame her own hair.

"Will you need a lift after work today?" Sara asked.

"Car's not fixed yet, so yeah. Thanks, girl. Good thing I'm working *your* shift this week. Yours is the only one around here that doesn't change. You're so lucky."

"See you at four," Sara smiled before they parted ways.

"Hey Gwen…" Sara stopped outside the open door of the administrator's office. Gwen Dames appeared to be buried in paperwork before she looked up at her friend.

"Hey There! Come in. What's going on?" She was always delighted to see her favorite nurse.

Sara advanced a few feet inside the room. "I was wondering if I can take about two hours lunch today. Have somewhere I need to go. I can get in here an hour earlier in the morning to make up the time."

"Oh, sure. No problem, Sara," Gwen waved a hand. "How's everything going, by the way?"

"Great. Everything's great," Sara answered.

"How are the kids… and Michael?"

"They're all fine. The kids, of course, are glad to be home doing—God knows what—during their summer break, and Michael... he's fine," Sara said, unsure of what else to say.

"Okay. Well, that's nice," Gwen started fixing the papers on her desk. "Cora Brooks can handle things until you get back."

"Thanks, Gwen. I really appreciate it," Sara smiled.

Gwen Dames knew Sara well enough to know that she was probably lying about how things really were at home, particularly between her and Michael. She could never forget the day she found Sara in the restroom sobbing her eyes out and only admitting—after breaking down even further—that Michael had mistreated her in some way. From that day on, Gwen never liked Michael, but respected the couple's privacy and never brought up the matter to Sara again.

* * * *

At 1:15 p.m., Sara pulled into the parking lot of the Gaming Board. In her white nurse's uniform, her purse tossed across a shoulder and keys dangling in her hand, she walked inside the building.

"Hi. I'm wondering if my husband, Michael Cullen is here," she said to the young, slender brunette who was primly seated at the reception desk. Sara knew that Michael rarely ever left the premises for lunch.

"Hello, Mrs. Cullen. Just give me a moment to find out for you." She picked up the telephone and moments later, inquired of the person on the other line of Michael's whereabouts.

"He's in the cafeteria having lunch," the lady said to Sara while hanging up the receiver. "It's on the…"

"Fourth floor. I know. Thanks," Sara smiled.

She took the elevator and did a final fixing of her hair before stepping out onto the fourth floor.

The cafeteria was a large open area that practically took up the entire floor. People were either in line waiting for food or sitting at tables having lunch. In the far left corner of the room, she spotted Michael. He was sitting with a young lady.

Sara walked up to them as Michael was speaking with his companion. "Hi," she said, looking at both of them.

Michael looked up, visibly shocked to see Sara standing there. "Oh, hi," he said. "Ah… Sara, this is Hollie. Hollie, this is my wife, Sara."

"Nice to meet you," Hollie said to Sara in a pleasant tone."

"Hi."

"Well, come join us," Michael said to his wife, who for a brief moment was feeling a bit awkward.

"What brings you here?" He asked after Sara sat down; Hollie listening intently for her reply.

"I just thought I'd pop by so that we can have lunch together," Sara said softly. "I wanted to surprise you."

"Well, what a pleasant surprise." Michael tried his best to sound like he meant it.

"I'll go to another table and leave you two to it," Hollie started to get up with her tray.

"No...you don't have to go. I met you here," Sara said.

"You really don't have to," Michael reiterated.

"Are you sure?" Hollie asked, looking at both of them.

"Sure. We're sure," Michael responded, Sara observing.

Hollie sat down again.

"Would you like for me to get you something to eat, honey?" Michael asked his wife.

Honey? Sara was surprised. He never called her that. "What do they have?" She asked.

"They've got great pasta, baked chicken, cabbage slaw - the works," Hollie interjected. "Why don't you and I go up there and you can see for yourself."

"Oh, okay," Sara was grateful for Hollie's kind gesture and the ladies got up and headed to the short line several feet away.

As they engaged in conversation at the lunch counter, Michael sat at the table alone, quietly fuming. *How dare she just pop up on me like that?* He thought. *How stupid! I could've been off the premises attending a meeting or conference, and she would've wasted time and fuel coming all the way over here instead of calling me in advance.* Nevertheless, in spite of how he really felt, Michael knew that he had to keep his feelings in check. He wasn't going to risk coming off as a jerk, especially in front of Hollie.

"So, how long have you been working here at the Board?" Sara asked Hollie as she placed a bowl of salad on her tray.

"Just a little over three months now," Hollie replied.

"Three months?" Sara was surprised.

"Yes."

"Oh, I just thought you might have been working here much longer than that... not sure why."

Suddenly, Hollie was quiet, sensing that perhaps Mrs. Cullen was wondering how her husband could be chummy enough to be having lunch with a newcomer. From that point on, the conversation had pretty much died and after Sara had made her selection at the counter, they rejoined Michael at the table.

"You're gonna eat all that?" He asked, inspecting his wife's tray.

Feeling somewhat embarrassed by Michael's question, Sara replied: "I've got salad, a little chicken and a pie. I don't think it's a whole lot to be eating right now."

"Absolutely not, Sara! I eat way more than that at every meal," Hollie said, defending Sara.

Just then, Michael realized that his plan of 'not coming off as a jerk in front of Hollie' seemed to have fallen out of the window.

"I was just saying… because I know you're always concerned about your weight and all," he said. *Oh man! I did it again!* He could have kicked himself.

Unsure of what else to say, Hollie started sipping her drink and Sara minced on her salad. She sat there feeling like the 'third wheel' as Michael couldn't seem to hide the *real him* even in public since he had practiced constantly being condescending at home so well. She was almost sorry that she ever showed up there like that and inwardly decided to never do it again.

After some awkward chattering, Hollie again told Sara that it was a pleasure meeting her and she left to go back to work. Michael remained a few minutes longer to see his wife off before doing the same.

"Are you angry that I came?" Sara asked him quietly.

Michael's face was now as stiff as steel—the way she was accustomed to seeing it. "I just wish you would have called; that's all." He took a sip of water.

"I understand, but I just wanted to surprise you," Sara replied.

"Well… you did. I have to get back to work now, so I'll see you home later, okay?"

"Okay," Sara got up and Michael followed. They silently rode the elevator together, Michael got off on his department floor and Sara continued down to the ground feeling like she had messed up once again. She walked out of the building much slower than she had initially walked in—not because she was tired, but because she was now depressed.

"Ready to go?" Beverley asked Sara who was sitting at the nurses' booth with a hand across her forehead, obviously deep in thought.

"It's four already?" Sara asked.

"Actually ten past," Beverley replied.

"Okay. Just give me a minute."

"Going to check on Sherlong?"

"He insists on it every day before I leave," Sara managed a smile that Beverley could tell took some effort.

"Okay, I'll wait here," Beverley said.

Sara walked down the corridor with arms folded.

"Freedom Queen…" Sherlong said, delighted to see Sara.

"Just wanted to let you know I'm leaving now," she said, standing at the door.

"What's wrong? You tired or something?" Sherlong picked up on her not-so-cheerful demeanor.

"Yes…very," Sara replied.

"Well then, you get plenty of rest tonight. You hear? Don't let that husband of yours keep you up late. You gotta be able to tend to me in the morning."

"I'll take your advice," Sara returned. "Have a good evening."

"You too, queen," Sherlong said as she was leaving.

"Ready?" Sara asked Beverley as she reached for her purse behind the booth.

"All ready," Beverley replied. They said goodbye to their colleague who remained at the desk and then headed out the front entrance of the hospital toward the parking lot.

Beverley was never at a loss for words. All during the drive, she went on about her life—car problems, cat problems and insomnia. She was menopausal and having a really difficult time getting to sleep most nights.

"I think I'm experiencing an early form of 'The Change'," Sara said, referring to the conversation of menopause.

"You think?"

"Yeah. I'm getting a bit moody and having some anxiety these days. I'm sure they're a couple of symptoms related to that stage."

"Yeah. They are," Beverley said. "Look Sara... I didn't want to bring this up 'cause I know how private you are."

Sara was quiet - kind of knowing where Beverley was heading with that intro.

"Is everything all right at home?"

"Sure. Why do you ask?" Sara returned, keeping her eyes on the road.

"You don't look so happy, Sara. I've noticed for a while now that you seem to have a lot on your mind most of the time."

"Maybe it's that pre-menopausal thing I just mentioned," Sara replied, uncomfortable with the topic.

"Maybe," Beverley said. "But I don't think so."

Sara sighed heavily. "Bev, I know that I confided in you once before about my and Michael's issues, but since then, we've been pretty good. We're getting on just fine; believe me."

"Really?"

"Yes, really."

"You wouldn't lie to me, right?" Beverley probed.

"You know I wouldn't, Bev."

"Okay... well maybe you are experiencing part of 'The Change' then. Let me tell you how you can tackle those mood swings and anxiety..."

Beverley went on to offer Sara a list of remedies for her apparent self-diagnosed condition and continued with the subject for the remainder of the drive. Sara soon pulled up in front of Beverley's house. It was a single-storey, yellow, trimmed white concrete structure near a cul-de-sac. Her blue sedan was up on blocks on the carport and immediately, Beverley was annoyed.

"That damn boy still hasn't gotten to it yet!"

"Tom's supposed to be fixing it?" Sara asked.

"Who else? You think I should have to pay *a stranger* to fix my car when my own grown boy is more than capable? These children today are really a piece of work! All that pain you go through to have them; you feed them; you clothe them; and when they grow up, they can't even be reliable enough to fix your bloody vehicle when they know how to?! How awful is that? He has me catching lifts up and down and he doesn't even have a job to go to! When he passes here tonight, his you-know-what is grass!"

"I'll see you tomorrow, Bev." Sara laughed weakly.

"Yeah. Thanks friend." Beverley got out of the car and closed the door. When Sara pulled off, Beverley was still grumbling as she made her way inside the house.

That evening, Sara retired to bed early. She had prepared dinner for her family, but didn't join them at the table.

5

"Are you all right, Mom?" Mira asked, walking inside her mother's bedroom after dinner.

"Oh, honey. Come sit here," Sara replied, reaching out to her. Mira went over to the bed and sat next to her mother.

"I'm doing just fine, honey," Sara said, rubbing Mira's arm. "I'm just a little tired; that's all."

"Are you sure, Mom? Are you sure it's not Dad?" Mira asked, much to her mother's surprise.

Sara sat up. "Why do you ask that, Mira? Your dad and I are doing fine."

"Mom, there's no use trying to cover for him. Both Wade and I can see that Dad doesn't treat you very well. He barely seems to notice you sometimes. Why do you let him treat you like that?"

Sara was momentarily at a loss for words. "Treat me like what?" She eventually asked.

"You know how he treats you. For one... you talk to him all the time and he's hardly ever listening; he's not affectionate towards you like some other men are with their wives."

"How do you know what other men are like?"

"I watch TV, Mom. Most men aren't like Dad. They're good to their wives. They talk to them, cuddle with them, play around sometimes - Dad doesn't do any of that with you. He doesn't even seem to *like* you," Mira explained.

Sara took Mira's hand and held it gently. "Your dad loves me, Mira. He loves you and Wade too—very, very much. He just isn't one to express his feelings; that's all. I know that sometimes his behavior seems cold..."

"Sometimes?" Mira interjected.

"I know, dear, but that's just the way he is. He doesn't mean anything by it. Believe me."

"I just wish he was different. It's not so much that he doesn't even say very much to Wade and me, but I just hate the way he treats you, Mom. I can't stand it." Mira was at the verge of tears.

Sara pulled her daughter closer and stroked her hair. "I'm fine, honey. I'm happy... really. I want you to believe that. All of us have so much to be grateful to your father for. He provides for us, takes such good care of us..."

"You work too, Mom," Mira indicated.

"Yes. But I only work because I want to, dear. I love my job. If it were up to your father, I wouldn't work because he earns enough money to sustain this family all by himself. By being a nurse, I get to take care of people and that's something I love to do, but I can retire tomorrow if I want to and your dad would not have a problem with that. So, trust me... he's a wonderful man. He may not say a lot or be very affectionate, but he loves his family. He loves us all very much and I want you to remember that.

"Okay, Mom," Mira replied, getting up. As she opened the door to leave, her father was heading to the bedroom. She briefly made eye contact with him, then headed to her own room.

* * * *

Mira got up to use the bathroom. The alarm clock on her night-stand read: 2:33 a.m. As she walked into the dark hallway, she suddenly heard a noise; it sounded like it was coming from the kitchen—as if a tin pan or pot had dropped onto the floor. With heart racing, she reluctantly forced herself to go have a look. She rounded the bend towards the front area, switched on the living room light and carefully proceeded into the kitchen. Scanning the floor, Mira was now confused about the sound she had heard—there was no evidence of anything having dropped—neither in the dining area.

Not knowing what the sound was and also not so keen anymore on finding out, she switched off the light and quickly headed to the bathroom. When she was finished, she walked out into the dark hallway again and headed to her bedroom. After crawling into bed, she reached over for the covers and on turning, her eyes met those of the mysterious, haggard woman she had seen before. The ghostly visitant was standing over her again with overwhelming sadness in her eyes and strangely, her entire silhouette glowed in the dark—the blood on her white dress eerily prominent. Though standing, she seemed to be floating several inches off the floor just as Mira had seen her in the closet of the Ferguson house. Startled and afraid, Mira quickly backed up against the head-board, knees raised, hugging them tightly with both arms.

"What do you want?!" She demanded in a shaky voice, staring at the apparition and hoping the thing would not hurt her.

"Have… you… seen… him?" The woman made a slight turn of the head.

"Who? Who are you talking about?" Mira pleaded.

The woman slowly raised her left hand, then suddenly, she was gone.

Wanting more than anything to dart into her parents' room as she had done before, Mira fiercely resisted. She remained against the head-board for what felt like hours—trying to digest the reality of what had just occurred.

As soon as the thought hit her, she sprung out of bed and hurried across to Wade's room.

"Wake up! Wake up!" She shook him vigorously.

Wade rolled over and cracked his eyes. "What do you want?" He asked lazily.

"I have to talk to you!"

"Can't this wait?" He asked.

"No, it can't," Mira sat next to him and switched on the lamp. "I've seen her again, Wade."

"Seen who?"

"The woman from the Ferguson house."

"What? Where?" Wade was now fully awake.

"She was in my room again!" Mira replied.

Wade rubbed his forehead and sighed. "What does she want? Did she say anything?"

"Only the same thing as last time. She keeps asking me if I've seen him. I have no idea who she's talking about. This time, I actually asked her who she was referring to and she just disappeared right in front of me."

"Wow. That's weird," Wade said.

"I'm afraid to be alone in there. I don't know why she keeps coming to me!" Mira was clearly frustrated. "Can I sleep in here tonight?"

"Okay. Let's just hope she doesn't come in here too," Wade answered.

Mira slipped under the covers with her brother and tried very hard to fall asleep.

* * * *

"That was a really awkward situation the other day." Hollie took a bite out of her donut.

"What do you mean?" Michael asked.

"Well… your wife showing up like that. You didn't seem that happy to see her." Suddenly, Hollie felt like she had wandered into waters she had no place veering into. "I'm sorry," she wiped her lips. "I didn't mean to get into your business like that. Forgive me."

"No. No… that's quite all right, Hollie. You're right; I wasn't happy to see her," Michael admitted, much to Hollie's surprise.

He sighed deeply. "Sara and I are not in the best place right now, you might say. We have some issues like every other couple out there does."

Hollie slowly stirred her orange juice with a straw. "Pardon my asking, but are you two trying to work out those issues?" She asked, for the most part still looking at the juice.

Michael cleared his throat. "In a way…yes and in a way… no," he replied.

Hollie stopped stirring and looked up. "What do you mean by that?"

"I mean that one of us is trying and one of us isn't."

"Which one are you? The one that is or the one that isn't?"

Michael reached for his water and took a sip. "I guess I'm the one that isn't."

Hollie was dumb-struck. Was Michael Cullen really coming out and revealing to her—a mere stranger—that he was having marital problems?

Sensing her shock, Michael said: "I know that doesn't sound good, but it's true."

"Your wife seems like a lovely lady, Michael," Hollie finally replied. "What could possibly be so bad that you don't feel like working out your problems?"

Michael placed both elbows on the table and clasped his hands together beneath his chin. "The thing is... nothing's so bad. Everything is good. My wife is a wonderful woman. I know she loves me, does everything for me and the kids, and tries really hard to please me... but as strange as this sounds... that might be the problem," he said.

Hollie was totally consumed by this incredible revelation. "Let me make sure I understand you. In essence, you're saying that your marriage is falling apart because everything is good?"

"No. My marriage isn't falling apart—that's not what I'm saying." Michael stretched out his arms on the table. "Sara and I are just having a bit of a struggle because in my mind I can't properly process, I guess, all the attention she gives me. It's always been that way and I think that the more time went by, I didn't know how to appreciate it anymore."

Hollie stared at him for a few seconds, hands clasped together on her lap. "Are you still in love with her?" She asked evenly.

"I love her," was Michael's reply.

63

* * * *

The sounds emanating from the motel room were only vague from the sidewalk. The thick, brown curtains had been drawn a few minutes earlier for reasons of privacy. A man's pair of black shoes and a woman's high-heel silver pair had been strewn across the floor along with a long, gray khaki pants, short-sleeved striped dress shirt, a silver mini-dress, and some underwear. The romantic interlude in the queen-sized bed was intense as the couple gyrated slowly beneath the thick blanket.

As the man looked deeply into the woman's eyes, he kissed her lips passionately and wished that the moment would never end.

* * * *

Feeling unusually tired, Sara had taken the day off from work. She had spent hours in bed wondering why she couldn't manage to pull herself together.

She walked into the kitchen for a glass of water and after looking up at the clock, noticed that it was 6:57 p.m. Thinking it odd that Michael wasn't yet at home, she sat down at the counter near the wall, picked up the phone and dialed his work number. The Gaming Board closed at 5:00 p.m., but Sara was sure that Michael was putting in a little overtime and had just forgotten to call.

"Security." A man answered the line after the third ring.

"Hi. Good night. I'm trying to reach Michael Cullen please," Sara said.

"Mister Cullen's already left for the day, ma'am," the officer responded.

"Really? Oh... I guess he's stuck in traffic then. Thank you, sir." Sara hung up the receiver with an uneasiness inside her gut. *It was strange for Michael not to call*, she thought. *What if he got into an accident?*

She walked over to the back door to see if it was locked. Wade and Mira were evidently in one of their rooms since Sara could clearly hear them arguing back and forth.

"Kids, keep it quiet in there!" She hollered before heading back to her bedroom. Just then, she heard a car pull up on the driveway. With a huge sense of relief, she turned and walked over to the living room window. Michael was closing the car door and heading inside with briefcase in hand. Sara proceeded to meet him at the kitchen door.

"Where have you been?" She asked before he barely stepped inside.

"I had to drop off some documents after work," Michael passed her, heading over to the couch.

"Don't they have a messenger for that?"

"Sure, but I decided I would take the documents to the vendor myself." He looked up from the chair—eyes reprimanding her for having the nerve to conduct that line of questioning.

"I was worried that something might have happened to you," Sara said, wanting to ease the rapidly building tension.

"Why? Because I got home an hour later than usual? Come on, Sara! That's crazy!" Michael kicked off his shoes. "Next time I decide to make a quick stop after work for any reason at all, I'll make sure to call; okay?"

Choosing to ignore Michael's sarcasm, Sara said, "I'll get your dinner now."

"Um… that's okay. I had a late lunch, so I don't need anything right now." He got up and walked off.

Sara stood there watching as he retreated to their bedroom without even bothering to check on the children.

Around midnight, Michael shot up in bed suddenly. His scream had awakened Sara who immediately sat up beside him.

"What's wrong? You had a nightmare?" She asked.

"Yeah," he returned in a soft whisper before slowly bringing himself to lie down again. His eyes, by then, had lost all desire for sleep.

6

_____

"Y ou look terrible!" Dwight Bridges handed Michael a file.

"I feel like a twenty-ton truck ran over me," Michael said from behind his desk.

"Preston McAffee's coming in at 10:30, so I suggest you grab yourself a cup of coffee or something... and quick? Wouldn't want the C.E.O. to see you looking like that. Would you?"

"I'll be fine," Michael's voice was almost dragging.

"How are Sara and the kids?"

"They're doing well," Michael rubbed his neck.

"That's great! Give them my love and I'll see you at the meeting," Dwight pointed.

Michael took Dwight's advice and had his secretary, Lima, bring him in a hot cup of cappuccino. For the most part, it seemed to have done the trick. Around 10:25, he grabbed his coat from the rack and headed out to the meeting. Stepping inside the conference room, he noticed that most of the executive board was already present—Dwight included—and Hollie was seated right next to him with legal pad in front of her and a pen fixed firmly between her slender fingers. Michael glanced her way, careful not to pique anyone's curiosity.

Taking a seat a few chairs down from Dwight, Michael looked at Hollie again. She was now looking back, but cautious also not to arouse suspicion.

As the meeting commenced and the C.E.O., Preston McAffee, a lean, bald sixty-year-old spoke, Michael's mind was occasionally distracted by thoughts of Hollie and their romantic rendezvous the evening before. They had both taken off from work a couple of hours earlier—Hollie's excuse was an impromptu doctor's visit and Michael didn't need one.

Hollie was just as distracted, but fought harder to focus since she was responsible for recording the minutes of the meeting. The whole affair thing was new to her and definitely a first, and she wasn't so sure how to feel. She did know that she was attracted to Michael and decided she would have to see how it all progressed.

After the meeting, Michael hinted by a slight shift of the head for Hollie to follow him. She trailed him down the hallway and off into a long, narrow corridor that led to the janitor's closet and some restrooms. Michael stopped short of the restrooms and pulled Hollie into the vacant janitor's closet where he held her closely and locked his lips onto hers.

"Did you think about me last night?" He soon asked, caressing her face.

"Just all night," Hollie replied, reaching up to kiss him again.

"I just had to hold you. It's all I thought about in the meeting."

"Me too," Hollie said.

"Can we get together later?"

"Can't. I promised my sister I'd watch my nephew tonight. I'm sorry."

"Don't be sorry." Michael smiled. "We have plenty of time to get to know each other better. We'll see how tomorrow goes."

"Okay," Hollie responded, feeling the tingly sensation she remember having one time ago—this time, with a slight mixture of guilt.

After one last smooch, Michael peeped out into the corridor before walking out into the main area. Hollie followed a few minutes later after freshening up in the restroom.

* * * *

There was a knock at the kitchen door. Mira, who had been watching TV in the living room, got up to answer it.

It was Monique Constantakis—the grand-daughter of one of their neighbors. She was a skinny fourteen-year-old with long candy curls and a few freckles spotted her cheeks.

"Hi, Mira," Monique said, hands shoved inside the pockets of her shorts.

"Hey. Come inside." Mira led the way to the couch as Monique shut the door behind them.

"So what're you doing?" Monique sat next to her friend who had both feet in the chair.

"Just watching TV."

"Where are your folks?"

"At work." Mira was not a very good conversationalist and Monique had pretty much accepted that fact. "So you're here for the weekend?"

"Na. Mom's picking me back up this afternoon. She had to run a few errands, so I got her to drop me off by Nana and Papa until she's all done. I wasn't into all those boring stops she said she had to make."

Mira re-focused her attention to the television screen. *Bonanza* was on and she so loved Miss Kitty.

"I wanna be as beautiful as Miss Kitty when I grow up," Monique said.

"Yeah. Me too… and classy," Mira replied.

The girls sat quietly for a while watching the program until Wade came out of the bedroom. He hailed

Monique briefly and headed into the kitchen. Sliding open the top drawer, he pulled out a used plastic bag.

"What are you doing?" Mira asked him.

"I'm going to pick dillies and mangoes over at the Ferguson property. Wanna come?" Wade said.

Mira shook her head. "No. I'm staying here."

Monique looked at Mira. "Why don't you wanna go? Come on! I wanna go."

"Well you two go then. I'm staying home," Mira was mercilessly firm.

"She's not coming, Monique," Wade said, knowing his sister would not be swayed after all that had happened. "If you wanna come, you can."

"Okay. I'll see you later, Mira." Monique stood up to leave.

Mira looked at Wade. "Wade, can I see you for a moment in the back?" Her voice was stern.

Monique watched them disappear down the hallway.

Mira walked into her parents' room and Wade behind her. She closed the door quietly and looked her brother squarely in the eyes: "Don't mention a word to her about what happened. You hear?"

"Sure," Wade answered, knowing that Mira meant business.

"If you ever tell anyone about that, I'll never speak to you again, Wade Cullen." Mira attempted one last threat to seal the deal.

71

"Stop tripping, girl. I won't tell anyone," Wade said before leaving the room.

Monique was still standing in the living room when Wade re-emerged a minute later. "Ready?" He asked.

"Yes!" She said, following him.

The children slowly walked the short distance to the Ferguson property where Monique gladly took over Mira's role of holding the bag while Wade dropped the fruits down from the tree.

"Why didn't Mira wanna come?" Monique asked him as he threw down the dillies.

"Don't know. Guess she doesn't like coming here that much anymore," Wade answered.

"You guys going to the carnival this year?"

"I guess me, Mira and my mom will go—we usually make it there before the carnival leaves."

"Not your dad?" Monique asked.

"My dad doesn't go much of anywhere—mainly to work and home. He isn't into too many things; you know?"

Monique nodded.

"Are you and your parents going?" Wade asked.

"Yeah—tomorrow actually. I remember when I was younger, I used to look forward to the carnival every year. I counted the days from a full two months ahead. I just loved it."

"And now?" Wade dropped another dilly which Monique had to lean over and pick up off the ground.

72

"Now... not so much. I still like going, mind you, but it's not the same hype that I used to have about it before."

"I know what you mean." Wade started down the tree and headed over to another.

* * * *

3:32 a.m.

Michael was awakened by a loud whisper at the tip of his earlobe. He slowly opened his eyes and what he immediately saw consumed him with such dread that he thought his heart would instantly fail him. A woman dressed in white was floating above his bed with arms extended widely. The look of terror filled her dark, veiny eyes that were stark wide and piercing him with a raging glare. Michael found himself speechless as the apparition hovered over him for what seemed like forever. He couldn't recall the words that had been whispered to him—that had awakened him—and now silently, he watched as slowly and progressively, the woman floated farther and farther away until she completely vanished into the eastern corner of the wall. The whole time, her eyes stayed on him. Michael was glued to the bed with the realization that it was the same ghastly figure that had awakened him the night before. Only, this time, upon seeing her, no voice would escape. He looked over at Sara who was lying on her side fast asleep. There was no way he could tell her that now he, too, had seen a ghost in their house.

He was afraid—very afraid—and just as the night before, sleep would not easily come.

Mira was in a deep sleep. The dream was unlike any she had ever had before. The land was huge. Cotton and other crops were being harvested by mostly young and middle-aged colored men and women. Some of them sang quietly, most didn't sing at all—almost none seemed happy. The women wore some sort of head-cloth on their heads, many of which were dingy and spotty in parts.

A young man stood out: Dark skin, rather muscular, of average height—very handsome—somewhere in his twenties. He was chopping wood a good distance away from most of the others. His large, muscular arms wielding the pick-ax made his job look easy.

The door of the large house opened. A young, colored lady with perfectly sculpted facial features, shoulder-length, black hair, and a slender physique stood in the doorway looking over at the handsome, young man. Their eyes met, but only for a moment, before someone called out from inside the house and the girl shut the door again quickly.

The tall, white, rather plain-looking lady, whose face was caked with make-up, had called out to the young woman. She was standing at the top of the stairs, telling the girl to fetch her bag, upon whose orders the young woman quickly ran up the tall stairway to heed. While passing the woman who had given the orders, she paid careful attention to slow down a bit in order to pay the respect that was seemingly due. The older woman, on the other hand, returned a look of utter contempt. The bag was handed to her and she was soon transported by horse and carriage away from the house and into the distance.

Then the dream shifted. A tall, domineering figure of a man with white hair was leading the young, colored woman—who seemed reluctant to go with him—into a large bedroom at the top landing of the house. He shut the door behind them.

* * * *

The next morning, Sara was up early preparing breakfast. Michael, still in pajamas, joined her in the kitchen.

"Morning. Any coffee?" He asked tiredly, sitting on a stool.

"You're not drinking your herbal like you usually do?" Sara asked. "Want me to put on a pot of coffee instead?"

"I really need coffee right now," Michael replied. "Otherwise, I don't think I'll have the energy to even dress for work."

"Didn't sleep that well, huh?" Sara started making the coffee.

"I couldn't get to sleep for hours," Michael said, sliding a hand through his hair.

"Oh, my. I'm sorry, honey. I'll mix this batch a little strong so you can get a good perk up, okay?"

"Thanks," Michael answered, appreciating Sara's concern.

"Morning, Mom and Dad." Mira entered the kitchen.

"What? Mira... is that you?" Sara was shocked. "What are you doing up so early?"

"I don't know. I couldn't sleep much longer. I know it's weird," Mira replied.

Michael looked at his daughter wondering if she, too, had seen what he had witnessed the night before.

Mira sat on a stool next to her father.

"You slept okay?" Michael asked her.

"Yes," she replied.

"Breakfast's almost ready," Sara said.

Michael wanted so badly to speak with Mira about the strange woman who had now appeared to both of them, but he dreaded even the thought of bringing it up. Sara handed him his coffee and he sat there quietly sipping it. Mira said very little as well as she watched her mother move around the kitchen. Then suddenly, standing directly behind Sara, almost touching, was the woman in white. Her head was extended approximately six inches above

Sara's and Mira could tell that as her mother stood there buttering a slice of bread, she was oblivious to the fact that someone was standing right behind her. The unwelcomed visitor looked at Mira and uttered in a deep, guttural voice, *"Have...you...seen...him?"*

Nearly falling off her stool, Mira cried: "Mom!" The stool tumbled over sideways and Mira darted off into the living room. On turning, she was relieved to see that the apparition was gone, but now her parents were looking at her in awe.

"What happened?" Michael asked.

"Honey?" Sara said, butter knife still in hand.

"Uh... nothing." Mira was still shaken, but at the same time not wanting to rehash any talk of ghosts with the unsettling probability that her parents might think she was losing her mind. "I'll... I'll just sit here." She sat down on the couch.

"What was that all about?" Sara probed, knowing that her daughter would not react in such a manner for no reason.

"It was nothing, Mom. Just don't worry about it; okay?"

Sara, neither Michael was convinced that it was *nothing*, but they also knew their daughter: Once she shut down on you, there was no way of getting her to open up. That happened only when Mira was ready.

Feeling more energized now that he had his coffee, Michael got up. "I'm going to get ready for work," he said, leaving the counter.

Sara just looked at Mira who was sitting in the living room now staring into space. She was starting to worry about her—her precious sweet pea who always tried to solve everyone else's issues, but who was also so good at keeping hers to herself.

* * * *

"Hey, Freedom Queen!" Sherlong exclaimed the instant Sara walked through the door. "How are *we* feeling today—as you often say?"

Nurse Jennifer Styles was in the process of giving him a sponge bath.

"We're doing fine." Sara stood aside, allowing Jennifer ample room to move around. "I see that Nurse Jennifer's taking really good care of you."

Sherlong looked up at Jennifer. "Yeah, Jenny here's doing a good job, but how about you give her a li'l well-deserved break and take over? My lower half hasn't been touched yet."

Jennifer shook her head and smiled. "You're a naughty old man; you know that?"

"Sure, I know," Sherlong responded proudly. "Freedom Queen over there knows just how I get down."

At that moment, a stocky, elderly lady with short hair and a round face entered the room.

"Good morning, Mrs. Sherlong," Sara said.

"Morning," the woman answered as if it took almost everything out of her to do so. Agatha Sherlong was a no-nonsense woman with a quick temper and just plain bad ways. The nurses were accustomed to her walking right past them without even bothering to hail. They thought old Mister Sherlong's philandering had probably turned his wife that way and so they didn't take her crude behavior personally.

"Did you get his pee pee yet?" She asked Jennifer out of the blue—not even bothering to hail her own husband.

"I'm getting to it, Ma'am," Jennifer replied, wanting to laugh out loud.

"You don't have to get to it nurse. That pee pee is mine and while I'm here, I'm gonna wash it!" Mrs. Sherlong was loud and direct, and Jennifer dared not protest.

"Mrs. Sherlong…" Sara intervened, "Nurse Jennifer will take care of that; there's no need for you to do it."

Agatha Sherlong swung around, her eyes glaring at the Head Nurse with undeniable ferocity. "How dare you suggest, young lady, that another woman washes my husband's pee pee? Have you lost your damned mind?" She walked briskly over to Sara. "That old coot in that bed," she pointed, "…is *my* husband. I am *his* wife. As long as

I'm around when he is getting bathed, I will wash his pee pee! You young girls just want what I've got. I know it ain't much lying on that bed over there, but it's still mine and I had better not ever hear you tell me again that another woman should wash my husband's pee pee. That pee pee bore me six children and that pee pee gave me much joy— so you had better know your place when it comes to my husband's private business!" She turned around and practically knocked Jennifer out of the way with her huge, rotund hips and took over washing her husband.

Sara did not mention another word about the matter and Mister Sherlong held his tongue as well. No one knew Agatha better than he did and he had learned after forty long years that you were better off not back-sassing his wife.

Sara left the room wanting to burst with laughter. She waited for Jennifer just outside the door and they both started walking and giggling together as quietly as they could.

"That pee pee gave me much joy..." Sara blurted softly.

"She called her husband a coot!" Jennifer added, holding her belly from the explosion that wanted to erupt. "Girl, I don't know how Mister Sherlong deals with that woman."

"And I don't know how Mrs. Sherlong deals with him," Sara replied.

The unusual episode lightened Sara's spirit. Earlier that morning, she had arrived at work feeling a little despondent about everything going on in her life, but Agatha Sherlong—unbeknownst to the crotchety, old woman—had lifted her out of that despondency - at least for a while. The less Sara thought about her problems, the better she felt and the more productive she could be on the job.

She walked into the hospital cafeteria about an hour later. Dr. Toby Lin was seated at a table eating a donut. He winked at Sara as she walked over to the server who was standing behind the counter.

"Good morning, Tia. May I have one of those, please?" She pointed at Dr. Lin's donut.

Tia pulled out a piece of clear wrap from the open box nearby and placed a jelly donut on top. "Anything to drink with that?" She asked, handing Sara the donut along with a napkin.

"A soda'll do," Sara replied.

"Soda in the morning?" Dr. Lin asked, wiping his lips and getting up from the table.

"I know, Doc. Just taking care of a little craving right now. I won't make it a habit; I promise," Sara said.

"I'll hold you to that." Lin waved a finger as he walked past.

Sara headed over to a corner table and sat down to eat her snack. The café was fairly empty that time of morning—one other person was sitting about ten feet away. Sara didn't know him.

"Want company?" Beverley asked, pulling out a chair.

"Sure," Sara looked up. "You're not getting anything from Tia?"

"No. I'm cool. So, what's crackin'?"

"Nothing's cracking, Bev."

"I'm gonna need a ride again today," Beverley reached over and broke off a small piece of Sara's donut and started to eat it.

"No problem. I just have to make a stop at the market on the way," Sara said. "What's Tom saying about your car?"

Beverley shook her head. "Nothing... absolutely nothing. I called a mechanic last night from an ad I saw and he's there dealing with it as we speak. That boy of mine is a piece of work. You know what he told me yesterday?"

"No. What?"

"He told me that he can't get to the car anytime soon because he's been having some strange pain in his groin area lately."

Sara stopped chewing. "Really? Did you check to see what might be going on with that?"

"Check for what? That boy's lyin' through his teeth. He ain't having no pain in his groin nor anywhere else. He's just lazy as hell!" Beverley was passionate, as usual, when it came to her son, Tom. She always blamed ex-husband, Joe for spoiling him rotten.

"How can you be sure that he's not telling the truth, Beverley? Tom could be in real pain which you, his mother, is ignoring," Sara said.

"Pain...my..."

Sara spanked Beverley's hand that was stretched out on the table.

"Anyway... Tom can fool one like you, but I know him better than anybody. He lies for a living—morning, noon, and night. I don't have time for anymore of his concoctions, so I put an end to all the crap and hired a real mechanic."

Sara decided to leave the subject alone; her friend was getting all worked up about it and the day was still too young for that.

7

Three days later

The young woman was locked in a loving embrace behind a small shed with the man who had been chopping the wood. She seemed to adore him and he— her.

"One day, we will marry," Mira heard the young man whisper in the girl's ear.

"Oh... Andy. That'll very well be the happiest day of my life!" The girl responded cheerfully.

They held each other for some time before the girl quietly snuck back to the big, white house. She entered in through the basement where there were two small cots. Mira sort of knew in her dream that an older female slave used to occupy the one on the right before she died and now the young woman slept down there alone. The girl started to undress when she heard a crack at the door. It was the tall, white man Mira had seen before in her dream.

The man rushed over to the colored girl, grabbed her by the arm and snarled: "You been sneaking around this property with that nigger boy; haven't you?!"

"I… I don't know what you sayin', Massa Cornelius." The girl was visibly frightened.

"You damn well know what I'm talking about!" He pulled her up to his face — the girl now in tears.

"I told you not to see that nigger no more and you didn't listen!"

"I did listen, Massa! I did listen!" She exclaimed.

"Come in here!" Cornelius hollered loud enough for the person standing outside the door to quickly enter. "Say again what you said to me, Frederick."

Frederick looked to be well into his forties or early fifties with strands of gray spaced through his black moustache.

"I saw them, Massa Cornelius. I saw them just now sneakin' lovin' outside one of the sheds in the yard.

"He's lyin'!' The girl cried in defense.

"No, you're lyin'. You know you been sneakin' lovin' outside that shed," Frederick fired back.

"I believe Frederick," Cornelius said looking the young woman in the eyes. "Tomorrow, there'll be no nigger for you to defile yourself with."

"No, sir! Please! I'll stop! I promise you; I'll stop!" She cried, oceans of tears flowing from her eyes.

"Get outta here, Frederick!" Cornelius demanded before releasing the girl.

Frederick stepped out immediately and headed back to his assigned cabin.

"I should take you out there and whip you like any other nigger!" Cornelius was furious.

"I promise you, Massa..." the girl pleaded, "...I will stop talkin' to Andy. I will never say another word to him again."

The towering man turned away. "You will never see him again."

"Please, Massa Cornelius! Please!" She begged behind him.

He stopped suddenly in his tracks and looked at her. He pulled her close to him again and spoke in a whisper. "I told you before you are special to me, Karlen. I told you I wanted you for myself—ever since the day you set foot on my plantation. I don't look at you the same as I do every other nigger. I look at you as a person. I... love you."

Karlen was momentarily at a loss for words, then finding her voice again, she said: "Massa... you say you love me?"

Cornelius hung his head down.

"But Massa, you have a wife and I am nothin' but a slave for you and your family. How do you love me when you have your wife?"

Cornelius looked at her again. "I just do. Don't ask me why. I will not have you givin' your heart to that nigger out there. I want your heart—I want all of you."

"I never heard of a white planter sayin' they love a slave before," Karlen added, hoping she had misunderstood what he was saying.

"I will spare that boy's life on one condition..." Cornelius started.

"Yes, Massa. I will do anything. Anything!" Karlen repeatedly bowed her head.

"You will never speak to him again; never kiss again; never lay with him again."

"Massa, we never lay together."

Cornelius raised his hand and slapped her in the face. "Don't you ever lie to me again; you hear me!" He yanked her by the arm. "I know you lay with him because Frederick said you did!"

"Frederick lie!" Karlen rebutted.

Cornelius shoved her onto the cot. "You do it again... and I'll kill him on the spot!"

He walked to the door, pushed it open and left.

Mira awoke suddenly, glancing over at the alarm clock that read 4:33 a.m. She sat up in bed and slid both hands through her hair. Events of the dream still lingered in her mind. She was beginning to think that her dreams of the young, colored woman were not meaningless dreams, but that perhaps, they were telling a story. She lay back down and stretched out thinking there was only one way to find out.

* * * *

"Get up!" She shook Wade who had not yet rolled over in bed. It was unlikely for Mira to be up before him and more unlikely for Wade to still be asleep when their parents had left for work.

"What?! What?!" He yelled, pulling the sheet over his head.

"Wake up! We gotta go!" Mira pulled the sheet back down again.

Wade turned over and cracked his eyes. "Why are you bothering me? Can't you see I'm still sleeping?"

"Not anymore. Get up!" Mira shouted at the top of her lungs.

Wade raised his eyebrows and rubbed his eyes. "Where are we going?" He yawned.

"We're going to Cornelius's house."

"The Ferguson house?" Wade needed to be sure.

"Yeah. So get up and get dressed!"

Wade sat up in bed, unsure if he was hearing correctly. "You said we're going to the Ferguson house?"

"Yeah." Mira was standing up.

"Why? Aren't you afraid to go back there?"

"She's trying to tell me something, Wade. I have to find out what it is she wants me to know."

"Who? The woman?"

"Yes. Her." Mira proceeded to tell him about her recent dreams and how she was sure they were telling a story.

"So why go there—to the house? Why not wait and dream about the rest of the story?" Wade asked.

"Because dreaming about it is not going to give this woman the help she needs. I have to go back to where I first saw her which is in that house. I'm not sure what's supposed to happen, but I'm being pulled there. That's all I can say."

Wade heard the passion in Mira's voice. "Okay." He started to get up. "Get outta here and let me get dressed then!"

Mira waited for Wade to wash up, use the toilet and get dressed. It took about ten minutes. The time was 9:07 a.m. when they headed out the door.

* * * *

Mira led the way up the trail to the huge, white house in the middle of the overgrown property. Wade had struggled to keep up with her—still amazed that his sister was returning willingly to that house.

Mira walked through the door, slowly making the turn that led to the winding staircase. She cautiously took each step upward while hearing the same cracking noise below their feet as they did last time. Soon, they were at the top of the landing and Mira walked into what she knew was the master bedroom as witnessed in her dream. Wade followed her, this time, far more afraid than she was.

She headed over to the closet, stood at the opening and looked inside.

Just as Mira thought, the woman in the white, blood-stained dress was there near the back wall—the same sad look in her eyes that she had always seen.

"Have… you… seen… him?" The woman asked again, reaching out a hand toward Mira. Wade was standing at the door next to his sister, but saw nothing.

"Who?" Mira asked the pitiful woman.

"Have… you… seen… him?" She went again, as if not hearing the question Mira had posed.

"Please give me his name," Mira said to the woman, whose arm was still outstretched.

The woman looked down and pointed at the floor. Suddenly, a moving scene came into view and Mira stood in amazement as before her appeared the likes of a large TV screen. It was as if she were watching a movie. The handsome, colored man she had seen in her dream came into focus. He was being whipped against a steel pole—his back sliced with every stroke of the lash inflicted by another negro while the tall, white man known as 'Cornelius' looked on. Mira saw the young woman, who in the dream was identified as Karlen, crying uncontrollably as she stood nearby watching the horrid undertaking. At that point, Mira looked up at the ghost who still standing in the far end of the closet. Her eyes were glued to the floor as the events partially explained her sadness. Mira looked down again and this time saw Karlen upstairs in the master bedroom of the large house with the man Cornelius and the plain-looking, white lady she had seen at the top of the stairs. Cornelius and the woman were arguing.

"I know you had been sleeping with her every time I turned my back!" The woman exclaimed. "Why don't you leave this nigger girl alone? I've had enough. I want her out of this house!"

Karlen was standing silently before them with hands crossed in front of her lap. She was visibly disturbed by the accusations.

"This is my slave and I'll do as I wish," Cornelius riposted. "She's not going anywhere, so you're gonna have to deal with it!"

The woman walked up to him and looked him squarely in the eyes. "Cornelius Ferguson, have you forgotten that you have a wife?"

Cornelius looked away, glanced at Karlen, then back at his wife with an intensity that she had never witnessed in all the years they were married. "I haven't forgotten, Marlena. I do, however, recall being the head of this here house and this entire plantation for that matter, and I'm gonna do as I damn well please. *You* will leave this house before Karlen Key ever does. You understand me, woman?"

Karlen was stunned by what she had heard her master say to his own wife. She knew it was because of his feelings, though twisted, for her.

Disgusted and appalled, Marlena walked off, then Karlen said: "No Ma'am. Don't leave. Please stay here." Then she looked at Cornelius. "I love Andy. I love him with all my heart and soul. Don't do this ungodly deed on the count of me a poor slave. Love your wife, Massa Cornelius, because no matter what you do to me or Andy, my heart will forever be his."

Cornelius stood there for what seemed like an eternity, staring at Karlen with a rage that soon consumed him. Not only had she admitted to defying him by continuing to involve herself with the field slave, but she had declared that her heart—the thing he, himself, desired most—would forever belong to the negro. With venomous anger, he yanked his pocket knife out of his coat pocket and lunged toward Karlen. On spotting the knife, Karlen screamed and ran into the walk-in closet as Cornelius's large frame had prevented her from escaping through the bedroom door. He ran behind her, Marlena, his wife, standing in awe as she watched the events unfold before her. Karlen was trapped at the far end of the closet with eyes open wide—the look of terror—when Cornelius grabbed her, pinned her against the wall, and stabbed her over and repeatedly in the abdominal region. Karlen's screams saturated the air, but no one in the house or even nearby on the plantation dared to venture upstairs to investigate. Cornelius continued stabbing his young slave moments after the life had already left her body. Marlena finally went to him and held his shoulders from behind as his vest and pants were covered in the blood of his victim. His short, white hair was disheveled and his sweaty face looked pained. When Marlena looked into Cornelius's eyes, she knew the eyes staring back at her were not those of her husband.

Shocked and chilled to the bone, Mira looked up at the woman who happened to be standing in the very closet in which she was murdered many years before. Mira looked down again and saw two field slaves carrying out Karlen's bloody body, wrapped in sheets, onto the plantation grounds where they buried her. The vision on the floor then disappeared.

Wade had stood silently the whole time as he knew that his sister was seeing something that he could not see.

"Tell me what to do?" Mira said to the apparition, wanting desperately to help her now more than ever.

"Have… you… seen… him?"

Suddenly, Mira understood. "Don't worry. I'll get him for you, Karlen," she said, before grabbing her brother's hand. "Let's go. We have to find Andy."

"Andy?" Wade was confused as they descended the stairway together; Mira cautiously holding onto what was left of the rail.

"Andy is the man she was in love with," Mira explained as they headed back to the road.

"You got a last name?"

"No, I didn't. But there must be records we can search through to see what we can find."

"Wait. Let me get this straight: We have to look for who?" Wade asked.

Mira filled Wade in as they walked back to their house. She was eager to find the missing link to the puzzle of Karlen Key's life and was certain that link would somehow free Karlen from the state of limbo she was apparently trapped in.

"But you described the scene as being from the slavery days. That was over a hundred years ago, Mira. How could you tell that woman ghost that you will find that guy for her? Shouldn't he be dead by now?" Wade was sure he was thinking more logically than his sister at that point.

"I know, Wade. I think that even if I find a picture or something of Andy, that it will satisfy her to some extent."

"A picture? You think they took pictures of their slaves in those days?"

"I don't know." Mira shook her head. "I just have to figure out something."

"We can check the State Records Office. One of my teachers last year said that they hold recent, but also very old records there on just about everybody. If you want, we can check it out," Wade said.

"It's worth a try," Mira replied.

Ten minutes later

"What in the world do you need to research?" Sara had picked up the line at the nurses' booth.

"I'll explain everything when you come," Mira said. "We have to get there before closing time."

"But honey, by the time I get home, the Records Office will be closed for the day."

"Well, I'm going to have to get there some other way, Mom."

"You will do no such thing, young lady!" Sara was adamant. "No child of mine goes wandering into the street on their own, especially at your age. When I get home, we'll talk about it, okay?"

Mira conceded, but her hopes were dashed as she knew she would not get to check the records that day just as her mother had indicated. Her thoughts were held captive by the ghost of Cornelius's house and inwardly Mira knew that she too, would not be free—at least mentally—until Karlen was.

* * * *

Feeling an air of urgency while on the phone with Mira earlier that day, Sara made a quick stop at the market that afternoon, then dashed Beverley home before driving home as fast as she could.

She walked in the door with a grocery bag in hand and Mira was standing there waiting for her.

"What's this all about?" Sara rested the grocery on the counter before proceeding over to the sofa where they would talk. Wade walked into the room and sat on the couch opposite them.

"Mom, I've seen the woman again… several times since I woke you guys up that night," Mira confessed.

"You mean… the ghost from Cornelius's house," Sara asked curiously.

"Yes, Mom. That's it," Wade interjected.

"You said you've seen her several times? Where?" Sara was apprehensive. "In here?"

Mira nodded, much to Sara's dismay. "She needs me to help her," she added.

"Come on, Mira. What is this you're saying? You're actually saying that a ghost needs you to help her?"

"Yes, Mom," Mira replied.

"Help her do what?!" Sara's tone was not so gentle anymore.

"Listen Mom," Wade started again, "I know this whole thing seems odd, but you and I both know that Mira wouldn't make up something like this. She's been having dreams about this strange woman and we were at the house today and the woman showed Mira exactly what happened to her."

"You went back to Cornelius's house even after your father specifically told you not to?" She was looking mainly at Wade because he was older.

"I'm sorry, Mom," Mira answered. "It's not Wade's fault; it was totally my idea. I had to go back there to find out what Karlen really wanted..."

"Karlen?"

"That's her name," Mira replied. "All she ever said to me was have I seen him."

"Seen who?" Sara was bewildered.

Mira explained everything to their mother; Wade dipped in whenever he felt he could offer something to the story. By the time they had finished talking and the shock of it all had, for the most part, worn off, Sara was reluctantly on board and said she would take the children to check the State's archives the next day which happened to be a Saturday.

"Whatever you do kids..." Sara started, "...don't breathe a word of this to your father. He would think we've all lost our minds!"

"Thanks so much, Mom!" Mira squeezed her mother tightly. "I can always depend on you."

"You're welcome, sweet pea," Sara answered.

8

Wrapped up beneath the covers at the Greenlight Motel where they had now adopted as their *special place*, Hollie wiggled her toes against Michael's. He was holding her in his arms and playing with strands of her hair.

"Michael..." Hollie started.

"Yes?" He whispered softly in her ear.

"What are we doing?"

Michael looked at her, surprised by the question. "What do you mean?"

"Why are we doing this? Is there any future for any of us in this?" She asked.

Michael wasn't sure how to respond.

"Do you love me?" Hollie asked.

"I care for you, Hollie. I care about you very much," he replied.

Hollie looked back at him. "You care?"

"Yes, I do."

"Okay… well, since that's the extent of your feelings for me, Michael, when I—on the other hand—am falling in love with you, I have to say that I don't think we can go on like this."

"Why do you say that?" Michael asked.

"Because if you are not going to leave your wife, I can't be tied down to you in your world. I have to move on and find someone who would love me and want more than anything to be with me. You caring about me is not enough." She sat up in bed and Michael followed.

"I don't wanna lose you, Hollie. Deep inside, I do more than just *care* about you. You must know that… but I can't lose my family. I can't leave Sara."

"Then I have to go." She got up and went into the bathroom, closing the door behind her.

Michael walked over and stood at the door. "Hollie, we can get through this. It doesn't have to end."

"Yes it does, Michael," Hollie answered weakly.

Instantly, Michael felt like his whole world was crumbling. His true feelings for Hollie had not been realized until he was faced with the prospect of losing her. He never thought it would be like this; he thought he had guarded his heart.

Hollie stepped out of the bathroom moments later, picked up her clothing off the floor and started to dress.

Michael took her hand and said, "Look, I'll do whatever you want me to do, just please give me some time. That's all I'm asking for."

Hollie sighed. "Michael... take all the time you need. Until you decide how much I really mean to you, we're not sleeping together anymore. It's just wrong and I can't live like this."

She picked up her purse and walked out of the room leaving Michael alone to ponder those last chilling words.

He arrived home at around 7:30 p.m. and had called Sara earlier to let her know that he would be late. When Michael walked inside, he saw Sara and the children sitting in the living room watching television together.

"Hi everyone," he said dryly, resting down his briefcase.

"Hi, honey," Sara got up to greet him. "How did the meeting go?"

"It went okay. We discussed a few things that were on the agenda, but will have to get to the rest sometime next week," he lied.

"Was Hollie there?"

Her question had caught him off guard. "Hollie? No... she wasn't. Why'd you ask?"

"You said she works along with Dwight, so I thought she might've been at the meeting. She seems like a very nice girl," Sara noted.

"I guess," Michael took off his coat and Sara quickly retrieved it.

"What are you kids watching?" He asked.

Wade and Mira looked up, both somewhat surprised that he cared to know.

"Gunsmoke," Wade answered.

"I like Gunsmoke myself—any cowboy movie would do me just fine," Michael replied.

Sara, Wade and Mira all looked at each other, unsure of what to make of him that night. What they didn't realize was that he was missing them already and riddled with guilt. Michael Cullen was falling in love with a woman he might ultimately decide to leave his family for.

* * * *

A full moon lit the sky that night. Michael sat alone on the front porch long after Sara and the children had fallen asleep. The night was peaceful and serene—a lot like what he wished his life was like. Only, he realized it was, before he crossed over the threshold with a woman who was not his wife. There was no better time for him to clearly collect his thoughts and sift through them logically and meticulously. He thought about the times he and Sara used to spend together laughing and playing around when they were a young couple; how she always adored him. He couldn't understand her profound admiration of him—her love; her passion; her loyalty. In his heart, he was unworthy of all of that. He was not the least bit deserving. He figured it must have stemmed from his rough upbringing and the rejection by his parents. The show of affection was something alien to him before Sara entered his life and receiving it, after a while, seemed to be just as difficult as giving it. Sure, it was easy to put on a show at first while dating, but keeping the façade going proved impossible for him.

Suddenly, he heard a creaking sound. It was coming from his left. Michael looked over and saw the other wooden porch chair, slowly rocking on its own accord. Startled, he continued to stare as the back and forth movement seemed slow and deliberate—but by what means? He wondered.

Appearing inside the chair was the woman with the blood-stained dress. She continued the rocking motion and soon, slowly turned her head in Michael's direction. He jumped out of his seat and staggered backwards against the closed front door. She continued to rock and stare.

"My God...." Michael was able to utter. "...what am I seeing?" He was still backed up against the door.

The ghostly visitor got up, then in a flash, she was standing—floating—directly in front of him, just inches apart. Her stare was intensely fierce and Michael's eyes were glued to the red and green veins that covered the white of the woman's eyes. She stood there for what seemed like hours, before vanishing into thin air.

Michael held his chest, breathing heavily to the point of gasping. He had never been so frightened in all his life. As quickly as he could, he fumbled the door knob and slipped inside the house, making sure to lock the door behind him. He joined his wife in their bedroom and lay closely beside her, his arm across her side like he used to do many years ago.

On feeling her husband's embrace, Sara put her hand on his arm and smiled.

* * * *

"Come on kids! Ready to go?!" Sara yelled from the kitchen. Michael was still in bed, though awake.

"Yeah. Mom," Mira advanced with a small book-bag on her shoulder.

"Why are you taking that?" Sara was looking at the bag.

"Safe-keeping. What we find, I want to secure— that's very important," Mira answered.

Wade walked into the living room. "Has anyone seen my red sneakers?"

"Look under your bed," Sara replied. "I'm sure that's the Lost and Found department under there." She and Mira chuckled.

As Wade returned to his bedroom to look for his sneakers, Sara walked back to her room, leaned over

Michael and kissed him. "We're heading out now to run some errands, honey, so we'll see you when we get back."

"Okay," Michael mumbled. He pulled up the covers and turned onto his side.

Sara, Mira, and Wade all piled into the car. The children always looked forward to going out with their mother on the weekends to run errands. However, this weekend, they were on a special, private mission—one Mira was really looking forward to. She sat in the front passenger seat since Wade's turn had been the last time they were out.

Traffic was pretty much *non-existent* while they were en route to the Records Office. Saturday morning commutes were nothing like weekday commutes: In that town, you could get anywhere fast on a Saturday.

Sara pulled into the parking lot and swung into one of the many empty spaces behind the Records building. Mira got out first—Wade and Sara followed. As they walked around to the front entrance, Sara playfully tossed an arm around Wade's neck. At fourteen, he was the same height as his mother and Sara could easily pass for one of his peers as she didn't appear to have aged past her teenage years.

Upon entering the building, Sara headed straight over to an employee who had just finished assisting a mature couple.

"Hello, Ma'am," she said to the frail-looking lady dressed in black, who sported a pair of burgundy-framed eyeglasses.

"My name's Bertha," the lady pointed to the badge pinned neatly to the lapel of her coat.

"Pardon me, Bertha. I'm wondering if you can help me find some information."

Wade and Mira stood nearby.

"I'll certainly try, miss," the woman responded, her face didn't seem to have cracked a smile in years. "What are you looking for?"

"I… I'm not sure where to begin," Sara glanced at Mira, before resetting her focus on Bertha. "It was during the slavery era."

Bertha gave Sara a look that plainly read: *What slavery era could you possibly be referring to??*

Sara cleared her throat. She knew from the scant information they had to work with that their research might not be easy. "I'm wondering if you have a list of slaves that might have worked on a particular plantation," she said.

"Well…" the woman who prided herself in being prim and proper, glanced at both children, then back at Sara "…it would be nice if you had a date and name with which I can work."

"I don't have a date, but I do have the name of the plantation owner," Sara replied.

The woman raised her eyebrows and lifted her chin as if hinting for Sara to provide such details.

"The name is Cornelius Ferguson," Mira interposed.

Bertha looked at Mira and managed a half-smile. "Okay, that's good. We're actually making headway now. Follow me."

They followed her to the back of the large, spacious room where Bertha directed them to sit at the pine desk parked over to the side. Wade pulled two chairs from nearby for him and Mira, as Sara took the one already there. Another one was on the other side of the desk - obviously for Bertha.

Behind the desk were rows of filing cabinets and a fairly large machine tucked away in the far corner of the room. Bertha searched through the chronological lettering in one of the cabinets, then returned with a thick file in her hand.

"What you need is information pertaining to the history of the Ferguson house. I don't know how long you've lived here, but *Cornelius Ferguson* has been a household name around these parts for years. He was only the wealthiest planter in all of Mizpah. Didn't your grandma or grandpa tell you about him?" She asked Sara.

"Actually… no," Sara answered.

"What?! Well, where in the world have you been? I thought everyone knew about Cornelius Ferguson. Why, my great-grandma and Mister Ferguson were high-society friends back in the day." Bertha was obviously proud.

"Really? Well then, you should be able to provide us with all the information we need," Sara returned excitedly.

"Now, I don't know about that... but I'll do my very best." Bertha sat down in front of them. "It's amazing how the State has preserved such documentation after all these years. Let me give you a little history..." She went on and on about Cornelius's parents, siblings and gradually made her way up to his wedding. "He married this beautiful woman, Marlena nee Johnston." She had a photograph to show.

Upon seeing that, Mira was hopeful. They had all sat closely together to view the photograph of Marlena.

"Would you happen to have any pictures in there of the slaves they owned?" Mira asked, interrupting the woman's chattering.

"Why... I'm quite sure I do." Bertha flipped through the file and came across a fairly large 8x10, black and white snapshot. "This here was taken back in 1863 according to the inscription at the bottom. These were slaves that worked on the Ferguson plantation at that time."

Mira stood up to get a closer look. Then, one of the men in the photograph caught her eye. "That's him!" She pointed, showing her mother and Wade. "That's Andy right there!" She carefully looked through, but didn't see Karlen Key anywhere.

Bertha looked up at Mira with marked suspicion. "How old are you, child?"

"Thirteen and a half," Mira replied.

"How in the world would you recognize Andy Anderson? Didn't seem like you folks knew much of anything regarding Cornelius Ferguson's existence when you walked in here. Andy Anderson, after slavery was abolished, was a vocal personality here in Mizpah. Did they teach you that in school?"

"They must have..." Mira returned, daring not to disclose the real reason she was able to identify him.

"Do you have a picture of Cornelius Ferguson?" Mira asked.

"Sure. He was one extremely tall, handsome man. Here he is... "Bertha blushed at the sight of the photograph.

Sara looked at Mira whom she knew had instantly recognized the man in the image. He was just as Mira had seen him in her dreams and in the vision Karlen had shown her. In the photograph, Cornelius had been dressed in a fine, emerald green coat suit with a high collar.

"Tell us more about this Andy Anderson person," Sara said, wanting the loquacious woman to enlighten them in that regard.

Bertha put the file down and crossed her legs as if eager to share what she knew. "Well, the talk is that Andy Anderson was the boyfriend of this slave girl named Karlen Key. The only problem is that Karlen was apparently having relations with Cornelius behind his wife's back. When his wife found out, there was some arguing and cussing, I guess, that happened and the long and short of it is: The slaves later testified that Karlen was murdered by Cornelius and buried right there on the plantation. After Andy was a free man, he lobbied to have charges brought against Cornelius, but nothing was ever done. He even wanted Karlen's body located and exhumed from the plantation grounds, but that was never looked into nor permitted. He got arrested and jailed several times for harassment because he wouldn't keep quiet about the whole matter. Andy Anderson fought for the sake of Karlen until he had no more fight left in him. He went on to live a long life—well into his seventies or eighties—but rumor has it that he was a very sad man after Karlen was killed like that and justice never came."

"Would you happen to know where Andy lived after leaving the plantation?" Mira asked.

"No dear. That's where my knowledge of Andy Anderson stops. Would you like to take your time and look through these records?" She glanced at all of them.

"Sure. Thank you so much," Sara said.

Bertha got up and left them to it.

The Cullens spent the better part of an hour going through the file and reading up on information pertaining to life on the Ferguson plantation and everything else they deemed interesting. Sara purchased a copy of the photograph with the slaves for Mira.

As they were pulling out of the parking lot onto the main road, Mira said, "At least we got a picture."

"That's a lot," Wade replied. "I didn't think they took pictures back in those days."

"Apparently, they did," Sara joined. "That's amazing how they kept all those records from way back then."

"But we still don't know where Andy moved to after he was freed," Mira commented, rather disappointed.

"No. But what does it matter, honey?" Sara asked.

"I'm not sure, Mom. I just feel that we need to somehow locate someone he was related to. I can't explain it."

The three went to take care of some other errands before heading back home. As Sara turned onto their street, they saw Mrs. Constantakis, from a couple of doors down, walking her Chihuahua.

Sara pulled up alongside her. "Hey, Mrs. C. How are you doing today?"

"Hi, lovely lady. I'm just wonderful. And how are you two sugar dumplings in there?" Mrs. Constantakis was bending down a little and peering through the window. One could tell from the woman's features that she used to be strikingly beautiful back in the day, as she carried her pulchritude well into old age.

"Fine. Thank you, Mrs. C." Wade and Mira answered simultaneously.

"I barely see you people and we only live a few houses apart." Her voice was shaky.

Sara smiled. "That's really something. Isn't it? How are your grand-kids?"

"They're doing well. Monique was here the other day for a few hours. Didn't she come by to hail?" She was looking at Wade and Mira.

"Yes, Ma'am," Mira answered. "Mom wasn't at home yet."

"Oh, I see." Mrs. Constantakis nodded. "So where are you bunch coming from?"

Sara hesitated for a moment, knowing how nosy her neighbor was. "We started off at the State Records Office this morning to do some research, then we ran a few more errands and here we are…"

"State Records Office? For what?" Mrs. Constantakis asked.

"We just wanted to find out some information about the Ferguson property up ahead," Sara replied.

"Cornelius Ferguson's property?"

"Yes, Ma'am."

"Why didn't you just ask Mable?" The woman was amazed that Sara hadn't thought of it.

"Mable who?"

"Mable Ferguson! She lives a good ways up on the southern side of Cornelius's land. She's his grand-daughter. Has a house there on a small portion of the property. You know that land is acres and acres long."

Sara was shocked by the news; Mira and Wade too. Mira knew right then that Karlen had been guiding them the whole time through the perpetual blabbering of Bertha at the Records Office and now Mrs. Constantakis.

"Yes, Ma'am. Do you know what color her house is?" Sara asked.

"Color? You don't need no color. Her house is the only one sitting at the front southern end of that land. No one else is anywhere near her."

"Thank you, Mrs. C. Can I offer you a ride home?"

"For what, dear?" The woman was flabbergasted. "I need to stretch my bones. I keep telling Charlie he needs to do the same thing, but he wouldn't listen. You know how men are. But in the event that he stiffens up like a board right there on that bed and can't move a muscle, Nurse Sara Cullen is just a couple of doors away." She winked.

"We'll see you later, Mrs. C." Sara smiled and drove off. She passed their house and made the semi-circle detour back around to the main road. They were on their way to Mable Ferguson's residence.

9

Sara rang the doorbell. Wade and Mira stood anxiously behind her.

Mable Ferguson's house was a single-storey structure on slightly elevated land. The white, trimmed peach abode was encircled by a white, low-level wall with galvanized iron spikes on top.

A slender, middle-aged woman came to the door. She was dressed in a pink and yellow floral robe and had several rollers in the front of her hair. "May I help you?" She asked.

"Hi. I'm Sara Cullen and these are my children, Wade and Mira. We don't live far from here. I was just wondering if we can have a few moments of your time."

"What's this about?" The woman asked abruptly, unmoved by the fact that another female was standing there with her children—regardless of how innocent they appeared to be.

"It's about your grandfather, Cornelius Ferguson," Sara added. "Look, if you would be so kind to allow us just a few moments of your time, I can tell you why we had to come here."

The woman gave the request some consideration, then invited them inside.

They all sat in the living room. Sara, Mira, and Wade bunched together on the couch and Mable sat in a smaller armchair, facing them.

As if prompted by something otherworldly, Mira said to her mother, "Mom, can we just tell her what's going on?"

Sara was startled by Mira's suggestion, not wanting this woman to know about her daughter's odd experiences. "Are you sure, honey?" Sara sought confirmation—all the while, Mable looked on wondering who in the world these people were and what they could possibly have up their sleeves now that she so foolishly let them through the door.

Sara looked at Mable. "Ma'am, what I'm about to tell you... I, myself was shocked to hear when my daughter, Mira, told me. A short while back, she and her brother, Wade here trespassed on your family's land and came upon your grandfather's house. Well, Mira saw something—someone inside that house..."

"You've seen the black girl too?" Mable gaped at Mira.

"Yes, Ma'am," Mira answered softly.

"Oh, my." The woman shook her head as if disheartened by the revelation.

"I'm sorry, Ma'am. The children should've never ventured onto that property. They very well should've known better than that."

"She's searching... even after all these years. She's still searching," Mable uttered, close to tears.

Sara and the children were astonished by the woman's reaction.

"I always hated what my grandfather stood for," Mable continued. "I am a Christian woman, Mrs. Cullen. I don't approve for one second what my grandfather did to that girl and her boyfriend."

"You've seen her too. Haven't you?" Mira asked.

Mable nodded. "For most of my life. She has not appeared to me for a few years now, but I still see—as plain as day—the pain in her eyes, her blood-soaked gown. Whenever I close my eyes, I see her—if only for a second. I know that's why no one could live in my grandfather's house after he died. Karlen Key is haunting the place and has done so ever since he snuffed the life out of her." Mira watched as Mable took turns squeezing and rubbing the back of each hand as she spoke. "Some years ago, I reached out to some of Karlen's relatives and apologized profusely for my grandfather's actions. I know it pained them even more to know that he never faced prosecution and no official charges had ever been brought against him for what he had done to their loved one. But they know that my grandfather couldn't dodge God's justice. Karlen's family appreciated my taking the time and having the consideration to reach out to them. I was amazed by their level of compassion and forgiveness. After reaching out to them, I thought sure I would never see Karlen again, but I still did for a good while. I also reached out to Andy Anderson's surviving children. Andy was the gentleman Karlen was to marry had she lived. His family weren't so accepting of me though—seeing that I am Cornelius's grand-daughter and all. They said that Andy's entire life was destroyed because of my grandfather's actions."

"I'm sorry," Sara interjected. "But it's not your fault. You are not your grandfather."

"I know that, but I am a product of him, nonetheless. His blood runs through my veins—that's hard for folks who's been so mistreated to simply overlook. "

"Mrs. Ferguson, would you be willing to give us the address of Andy's relatives?" Sara asked. "Perhaps, by us reaching out to them and Mira telling her story, they may be ready to extend that forgiveness."

"I would be happy to."

Mable got up and went into a back room. She returned a few minutes later with a piece of paper in hand. "This here is his son's name and address."

Sara gratefully accepted the note and she and the children stood up to leave. "You are a wonderful person, Mrs. Ferguson. It was really a pleasure meeting you today."

"Likewise, Mrs. Cullen. Feel free to stop by anytime you have some free time on your hands so that we can get better acquainted. I don't get much visitors and it would be my pleasure," Mable replied.

They started out the door.

"Oh, and Mira..." Mable started.

Mira looked back.

"You and your brother... do take good care of yourselves."

"We will, Ma'am. Thanks," Mira said.

As they drove off, Sara, Mira, and Wade had a really good feeling that everything was going to fall into place just as it has been up to that point.

Feeling relieved, Mira said: "Are we going there now, Mom?"

"No, honey."

"Why not?!" Wade exclaimed from the back seat.

"We can't do everything in one day, kids. I have to go home and prepare dinner now. I didn't think we were going to be gone all day long. We'll go and pay George Anderson a visit after church tomorrow," Sara responded.

"We're going to church?" Wade asked.

"Yes. I know we've missed a couple of Sundays..."

"A couple?" Mira felt the need to interject.

"Okay... more than a couple." Sara admitted. "I'm not proud of our prolonged absence from The Lord's House, but we're going tomorrow, okay?"

"Cool," Wade said.

"Father Bob won't recognize us," Mira asserted.

"'Course he will," Sara smiled, pulling onto their driveway.

Michael was still in bed when Sara walked into the bedroom. The curtains were still closed and he was snoring lightly. His usual routine on Saturday mornings was going outside and doing yard work until Wade returned home to help him. Wade rarely ever passed up on the opportunity to get away from the house for a while. He and Mira shared that quality. But it appeared obvious to Sara that Michael did nothing all day, except sleep.

Not wanting to disturb him, she tip-toed out of the room and quietly shut the door behind her, then went over to Mira's room where the kids had started a game of cards.

"I just want you to know that your father is asleep, so please keep the noise down in here, okay?"

"Sure, Mom," they each answered.

Sara went to get dinner started. In a way, she was glad that Michael was asleep, so that hopefully, when he awoke, the food would be ready. As she worked, Sara's mind drifted onto the events of the day— Bertha in the Records Office, all the documentation they looked at, Mrs. C telling them about Mable Ferguson, and Mable being the link that would connect them to Andy's relatives. Reflecting on those events, Sara was certain that they were all in the Divine Plan where all the dominoes fell into its proper order down the line. She felt proud to think that her own daughter could be the one to help a poor, lost soul find the freedom that had evaded her for so long—in life and then in death.

Two hours later

When Michael came out of the bedroom, Wade and Mira were at the table finishing up dinner and Sara was at the sink washing dishes. He hailed the kids, then sat down at the counter.

"You're finally awake, sleepy head," Sara said to him, while putting a bowl in the rinse water.

"Was really tired." Michael's voice was groggy.

"You slept all day? We got here around 4:00 and you were out cold."

"Yeah. Pretty much."

"Hungry?" Sara asked.

"Very."

"Well, go over to the table. I'll bring you some dinner."

Michael went over and sat next to Wade. He shuffled the boy's hair before sitting down. Wade looked at his dad wondering if his real dad was inside that human body.

"Enjoyed your meal, Mira?" Michael asked as Mira ate her last forkful of pasta.

"Yes, Dad," Mira answered.

"What did ya'll do today?"

119

Sara looked over.

"Nothing special—just ran a few errands with Mom," Wade answered. "Are you feeling okay, Dad?"

"Sure. Why'd you ask?"

"No reason. You've been sleeping a whole lot today," Wade replied.

"Yeah, I was. I just felt so tired since I woke up this morning. I haven't been sleeping very well these past few nights. I think I might've only gotten about two or three hours each night for the past week."

"Really?" Sara asked. "I know you mentioned a couple of times that you hadn't slept well, but I didn't know this has been happening all week. That's terrible. What do you think is causing the insomnia?"

"I have no idea," Michael lied.

"Well, you sure made up for it today, Dad," Wade said. He was so happy to be sitting next to his father and actually having a conversation with him for a change. It reminded him of when he was much younger—of the times his dad used to show interest in him and Mira.

That night, sensing that her husband's rigid demeanor had floated off somewhere into the abyss for an unannounced period of time, Sara pulled out her black negligee—the one Michael used to love for her to wear. After a long bubble bath, and knowing the children had fallen off to sleep, Sara lotioned up all over and slipped on the light, sheer garment. She stepped into the bedroom where Michael was lying shirtless with a hand behind his neck, watching television. He looked her way.

"Wow! You look… beautiful," he said.

Sara had not heard Michael utter such words to her for at least a full decade. Right then, she too was wondering where the real Michael had gone and who was this inside Michael's rock hard body. She slowly advanced toward him and he quickly sat up, feet outside the bed. She stood in front of him and he stood up and held her closely in his arms. As he kissed her lips, it took him to a place he had long deserted, but fondly recalled. In recent years, their love-making had been replaced with mere sex, but tonight, the love aspect of the act was returning. In Michael's mind, he didn't know if their love-making that night was going to be the start of something new and refreshing within their marriage or if their love-making would symbolize the end of it.

"Where is my husband?" Sara asked, lying in his arms after a full hour of intense intimacy. She was whispering, *"Thank you, God; Thank you, God"* the whole time.

"I'm right here," Michael answered softly.

"It can't be. I'm ashamed to say it, but my husband is not this loving."

"He is now," Michael replied, not sure that he should have said that as he still hadn't decided what he was going to do about Hollie.

They eventually fell asleep in each other's arms. Michael's night was peaceful and uneventful.

10

"Wake up, kids! Remember we're going to church today." Sara felt buoyant that morning—almost like she was floating on air. She went back to her bedroom and into the closet, passing Michael who was lying awake in bed. She sifted through the clothing in order to make a selection.

"Can I go with you?" Michael asked, standing in the doorway.

Sara looked at him, disbelieving her own ears. "What did you say?"

"Can I go to church with you?"

"Are you okay, Michael? Did you find out you're going to die or something and just not letting me know?"

Michael managed a smile. "I don't *think* I'm gonna die right now, but you never know..."

"Oh, honey... of course, you can join us! We'll be so glad to have you come. The kids will be elated!" Sara went over and hugged him tightly. Suddenly, she was feeling desirable and appreciated again for the first time in a very long time. Michael had inexplicably transformed into the man she always wished he would become and she desperately hoped that side of him was there to stay.

* * * *

He sat on the pew next to his wife and children feeling like the worst person that ever walked the earth. Listening to Father Bob speak on love and respect was another nail in Michael's coffin. He wanted to block out everything and just focus on the *here and now,* so that in spite of the decision he ultimately made, at least he knew he was creating some good memories for a change after being responsible for so many bad ones.

Father Bob greeted parishioners at the door after the service. On spotting Michael, he reached out and shook his hand briskly. "Michael, it's great to see you again! How have you been?"

"I'm doing well, Father... and happy to be here today," Michael responded. Sara and the kids glanced at each other with a smile.

"How long has it been since you were last here?" the balding priest asked.

"Um... maybe about a year or two... or a couple more than that." Michael was clearly embarrassed.

"Well, it seems like I need to reserve a day or two for confession just for you, Michael. I expect to see you soon."

124

They all laughed and Michael felt that Father Bob may be right on the button. He hadn't been anywhere near the confessional in many years.

They drove away from church, each member of the Cullen family feeling like they were an actual family again—a team. Mira and Wade started joking in the back and Sara, in the front passenger seat, was talking Michael half to death like she usually did. However, this time, he actually engaged in the conversation.

A few minutes after leaving church, Mira said: "Mom, when are we going to do that thing?"

Sara looked back at Mira, then at Michael.

"What thing?" Michael asked.

Sara sighed. "Michael, we have to take a detour to 236 Moody Road."

"Why?" Michael insisted. "What's on Moody Road?"

"Someone we really have to see. Pull to the side for a minute. Will you?"

Michael glanced through his rear-view mirror and cautiously swerved to the side of the road near an intersection. Sara turned to face him.

"Honey, there's something I need to tell you..." She looked back at the kids to offer a hint of re-assurance. However, the expression on Wade and Mira's face indicated that they weren't sure they shared their mother's sentiments. "We haven't told you this, Michael, but Mira has seen that woman she told us about several times since that night."

Michael glanced back at Mira who was sitting directly behind Sara. "What woman?" He asked knowingly.

"The colored woman with the blood-stained dress," Mira said.

"Since then, Mira's even been having dreams and visions of what actually happened to this young woman," Sara continued.

Michael sighed, then came to a sudden, much needed release of his pride. "I've seen her too," he quietly confessed.

Everyone's eyes were on him.

"You have?" Mira was startled.

"Yes. Several times. She's appeared to me several times. That's why I barely got any sleep for the past few nights."

"Michael, why didn't you tell me?" Sara asked in amazement.

He shook his head. "I don't know. I guess I was ashamed to know that I, as a grown man, was afraid—of a ghost."

"What did she say to you?" Mira asked.

"Nothing… absolutely nothing."

They went on to explain to Michael the events of the previous day and how they were about to pay Andy Anderson's son a visit.

"But why do we have to see him?" Michael was confused.

Sara and Wade looked at Mira for the answer.

"I'm not sure myself. All I know is it's a strong feeling inside that tells me that he has to go to the Ferguson house," Mira replied.

"Did the ghost tell you that?" Wade asked.

"No. She didn't. It's just a strong feeling that I have."

"I thought we were going to Mister Anderson's house to sit and speak with him and then hopefully, try and get him to let go of the past in order to allow healing for himself and his family. I don't know... but my thoughts were that once they are able to do this, then Karlen Key can be at peace," Sara said.

"Karlen Key?" Michael was puzzled.

"Yeah. That's the name of your ghost," Sara smiled.

"Mom, where did you get that scenario from?" Wade asked sarcastically.

"Well, what did you think?" Sara probed.

"I wasn't thinking any of that. I figured that Andy's son would have the answers."

"Mira, why didn't you share this with us sooner?" Sara asked.

"I wasn't sure, Mom, until this morning. I was thinking of it for the most part of yesterday, but wasn't sure if it made any sense. But when I woke up with it on my mind again this morning, I just knew that Mister

Anderson's son has to go to the Ferguson house. He just has to."

"How in the world are we going to convince this man—we being mere strangers—that he must walk into the house of the man he probably despised most in this world? How do you suppose we do that, Mira?" Sara posed.

Mira was quiet, then she said, "I don't know."

The Cullens pulled up at 236 Moody Road in front of a two-storey, run-down wooden structure.

Michael decided to go to the door and introduce himself first before inviting the others to come out. He knocked at the door and waited. Thirty seconds later, he knocked again and waited. Then, on impulse, he walked around to the side of the building where he spotted a much older gentleman smoking a cigarette on the back porch. Michael could tell that he was well into his eighties.

"Who are you?" The man asked bluntly before Michael had a chance to say anything. "Everyone who knows me know where to find me. What you want?" He didn't bother to look in Michael's direction.

"Pardon me, sir, but are you Mister George Anderson?" Michael asked.

"Who's asking?"

Michael cleared his throat. "My name's Michael Cullen. I was wondering if you can spare me a minute."

The man didn't respond.

"It has to do with your father and a woman named Karlen Key." Michael assumed that he was, in fact, speaking with George Anderson.

The man's facial expression seemed to have softened somewhat at the mention of his father and Karlen. He turned and looked at Michael. "Go on."

"My daughter has something she needs to say to you, sir." Michael wasn't sure where those words came from. "If you don't mind, I'll ask my family to come out—they're in the car."

He nodded with approval.

Relieved, Michael went around to the front and waved to the others who were looking in his direction. One by one, they mounted the porch and exchanged pleasantries with Mister Anderson. There was only one chair on the porch and George unabashedly remained in it. He focused his attention mostly on Mira who was standing there with the small, green book-bag in her hand.

"You have something to say to me?" He asked her.

Mira looked up at her father, realizing that he had set the stage.

"Um… sir, I have to say this first," Sara intervened. "We would really appreciate if you just have an open mind to what you're about to hear. We're not strange people; we're ordinary people who don't make up wild stories for attention. What our daughter, Mira here, has to say to you is the God's honest truth and I hope you accept it as that." She stepped back a little and waited for Mira to explain.

George nodded, then refocused his attention on Mira.

"Sir, I know how much your father, Mister Andy, loved Karlen. Karlen's still trapped in the vicinity of the Ferguson plantation—mainly in Mister Cornelius's house in the closet where he killed her."

George Anderson leaned in closer, startled by what the girl had said.

"Karlen has been appearing to me, sir. I've also seen her and Mister Andy in my dreams and she showed me by way of a vision why and how she was killed. She's looking for your father, Mister Anderson. She's been looking for your father on that plantation for many years."

George looked away as if in deep contemplation.

"Sir, I am not lying to you," Mira continued. "We all just came from church and I dare not lie on The Lord's day. Everything I said is true." She pulled the copy of the photograph she had gotten from the Records Office out of her small book-bag and handed it to George.

George's eyes welled with tears as he looked at the photo.

"Isn't that your father?" Mira asked.

George nodded.

"Karlen really loved him, Mister Anderson. She still does—even to this day," Mira averred.

The tears were flowing even heavier now. George looked at the other members of the Cullen family, then again at Mira. "I believe you, child. Karlen Key was all my father spoke about most of the time when he bothered to talk—Karlen this, Karlen that. Even while he and my mother were married and down to the time of her passing, he brought up Karlen's name. He never got over the woman. One time, he told me that she was his first true love. My mother, humble as she was, understood that this woman was before her time and she couldn't do nothing about my father's feelings, so she accepted it. She accepted him and loved him, and also grew to love the Karlen he so often spoke about. My sister and me got paid a visit from Cornelius Ferguson's grand-daughter one time ago. She was really sorry and sounded like she wanted our forgiveness. We knew it wasn't her fault, but when she showed up here, it was so close to the time after our daddy passed away and we was still reeling from knowing he died of a broken-heart. Cancer came on him because of his broken heart, but it wasn't the cancer that killed him—it was Cornelius Ferguson. It was him taking his Karlen away from him like that and getting away with it."

Everyone stood quietly, not wanting to interrupt.

"So little girl... I believe you and I'm sorry Karlen's still stuck on that God-forsaken property, but my father's gone now. He passed away years ago."

"Sir," Sara started, "Mira seems to believe that if you go to the Ferguson house it will somehow help Karlen in that state she's in."

"Me?" George pointed to his chest. "How can my going there help her in any way? I am not my father. Besides, I never want to step foot in that house or on that land where my father worked his hind off and was beaten down like a dog back in the day."

"Mister Anderson, do you believe... and I mean *really* believe everything my daughter has told you so far?" Michael asked.

"Yeah. I know the little one told the truth," George replied.

"Well, all I ask is that you trust that she knows what she's saying about you needing to go to that house. I admit, we don't know how your presence would help—none of us do—not even Mira here, but if she says it will, we're inclined to believe her."

George took his time considering the whole scope of the matter. The Cullens stood patiently, understanding how difficult the decision must be for him.

"All right," George finally said. "I'll do it. When do we go?"

Michael looked at Sara and Sara at Mira.

"We don't want to impose on you, Mister Anderson. You tell us when you'll be ready and we'll come back for you," Michael stated.

"How about now?" George proposed.

"Now? You wanna go now?" Michael returned.

Wade and Mira were smiling and so was Sara.

"Let me grab my hat from inside and I'll meet you out to your car. Any space in there?" He asked.

"Yes, sir. We'll make space for you," Michael answered.

"Thank you so very much, sir," Mira said as George turned to enter in through the back door of his house.

George Anderson turned around, walked out and pinched Mira's cheek. "You're a special young lady. You know that?"

"Yes, sir." Mira smiled.

"No wonder she appeared to you, 'cause she was special too," he said.

"I guess that makes me special also." Michael couldn't resist.

"You saw her too?" George asked.

"Yes, sir." Michael smiled.

"I see. Anyway, let me get my hat." George was careful to take his time moving around as his knees occasionally bothered him. Years of manual labor at the Tyroon Factory had taken a toll on his joints. Aside from that, he was in remarkable physical condition for a man his age.

Wade and Mira bunched up together in the back seat leaving sufficient room for George. Michael had waited on the back porch for him while the others went to the car. As he and George approached the vehicle, Michael went ahead and opened the door to the side directly behind the driver's seat. George carefully got in, resting his cane next to his leg.

During the drive, the elderly man filled the family in on many things his father had shared with him throughout the years. The Cullens were humbled to be educated by the son of a man who had fought relentlessly—against all odds—for the cause of his murdered soul-mate. They were astonished by some of the mistreatment Andy was said to have suffered on the Ferguson plantation before and especially after Karlen Key was killed.

11

"This is gonna be a long walk," Michael said after they all got out of the car. He had parked as far in on the land as possible for George's sake.

"Are you sure you can walk this distance?" Michael asked him.

"I have my cane here, so I know I can make it," George replied. "If I get tired or the knees hurt, I'll just take a short rest." He was wearing a straw hat, a plaid shirt and dark-brown trousers whose age and numerous washings were obvious even if you didn't give it a good look.

They started through the wooded area. Mira and Wade walked ahead while Michael, Sara and George trailed behind them. George led the conversation the whole time, but Michael was hoping all that talking would not weaken the old man significantly.

"How much further?" George asked, taking his first break by leaning against a low brick wall that encircled a well.

"We still have a good ways to go, sir. Just rest here as long as you need to," Michael replied.

"I don't need much rest. For the most part, I'm in tip-top shape. It's just these knees of mine that give me trouble from time to time; that's all."

"I understand," Michael said.

Seeing the adults had stopped, Mira and Wade waited where they were until George was ready to continue.

After climbing the porch of Cornelius's house with his tattered cane, George hesitated in front of the open doorway. Mira and Wade had already walked inside and were waiting in the great room for the others.

"Are you all right, Mister Anderson?" Sara asked.

"Yes. Yes." George nodded, as he often did and then he walked inside.

Immediately, Mira's attention was captured by the doorway just beneath the arch that led into the kitchen. Karlen Key was standing there, as if with great anticipation.

After walking in behind Sara, Michael noticed her too.

"Do you see her?" Mira asked, referring to no one in particular.

"I don't see nothin'," George was looking around.

"I see her," Michael affirmed, eyes affixed to the ghostly image that had frightened him beyond expression.

"A....N....D....Y..." went the deep, guttural voice that echoed loudly into the air.

Sara grabbed her husband's arm as she had heard the voice of the woman she could not see. George had heard it too and was moved.

Wade, aghast, stood close to his parents.

"I... I'm not Andy," George responded, voice cracking. "I'm his son, George."

Mira was still staring at the woman who had now raised both arms and extended them as if in a welcome pose. She was looking straight ahead into the distance.

"A....N....D....Y..." she went again. Michael looked on, holding firmly to his wife and she to him. Karlen's dark, veiny eyes, to him, were most frightening.

Suddenly, a young man dressed in a brilliantly white suit entered the room. Around him was a glow that was almost blinding. He seemed to be walking on air. Karlen made her way toward him with outstretched arms and then, in an intensely profound moment in time, the two embraced for what seemed like centuries. The room around them appeared to be spinning and soon, George, Sara and Wade could see them too.

"Daddy...." George uttered as the couple was still locked in their embrace. "My God... it's him. It's him when he was younger. He looks so handsome and... peaceful now."

Tears were streaming down Sara's face and when she looked up at Michael, she saw that he was crying too.

She held him even more closely as it was the first time she had ever seen him cry. Wade was entranced by what he was seeing and Mira stood closest to the apparitions with a smile of overwhelming relief on her face.

After Andy and Karlen separated, they were holding hands, but Karlen's features had also changed. She was young and beautiful, and was wearing a dress such as that of a princess. It was as white as snow; there was no more blood. Her eyes were bright and clear, and her hair, black and silky in texture. She and Andy were both the same ages as they were when they first fell in love.

Karlen looked at Mira who was standing six feet away from her and with a radiant smile, uttered, *"Thank you."*

Mira was still smiling from ear to ear when Karlen looked over at Michael who was still looking at her and crying uncontrollably. This time, Karlen's stare was one of approval. Michael broke down even more, Sara and Wade both held him—amazed at how sentimental he had become.

Michael looked at his wife and pulled both of her hands up to the level of his chest. "I love you, Sara. I love you and the kids with all my heart and soul. I'm so sorry for all the hell I put you through. I'm so sorry, Sara. Please forgive me; please! I promise, I will be a better husband and father. I promise! Just please, please forgive me!" The more he spoke, the more he cried. Michael realized at that moment in time that Karlen Key had been trying to save him by appearing to him the way she did. She didn't want him to destroy the marriage he had been blessed with. She wanted him to treasure and preserve his family.

Karlen nodded slowly, then started to walk with Andy into the distance. George, Sara, Michael, Wade, and Mira all watched as the unearthly couple walked on air for at least fifty feet, then disappeared before their eyes.

Michael was still crying and Mira went over to comfort him as well. "We forgive you dad," she said.

"Yes, we forgive you," Wade agreed.

Then Sara looked into Michael's eyes, cupped his face with her tiny hands and said, "I forgive you, honey. I will love you with a love that never dies—the kind of love Karlen Key has for Andy."

George had shed a few tears as well. Seeing his father like that gave him such peace in his heart.

"He was with you all the while." Mira went over to George. "That's why when you came here, they were able to find each other. I understand that now."

They all looked at her and felt that each of them had made a positive imprint in a history that had been racked with bad memories. With that in mind, they knew that Mira had made the greatest impact. She was chosen by a young woman, who had long been lost, to find freedom for her and ultimately in the process, they all—in some way—were freed.

Mira walked toward the front entrance.

"Where are you going, honey?" Sara asked.

"Off of this God-forsaken property. Karlen's not here anymore and we no longer need to be."

They all managed a weak laugh and headed out behind her.

Outside on the ground, Michael looked back at the house, knowing that he will always remember the very special lady who had saved his family... and in essence— his life.

The very next day, he ended his affair with Hollie and a few weeks later, she landed a secretarial job with a new agency on the other side of town. Michael never saw her again.

* * * *

One month later

There was a knock at the door.

"I'm coming!" Mable cried, drying her hands with the dish-cloth.

The knocking continued.

She opened the door widely, ready to bark at the individual that seemed determined to put a dent in it. Then standing before her—on her very own porch—was the one person in the world she never expected to see. It was

George Anderson. Sara Cullen was standing right next to him smiling.

George opened his arms widely and stepped forward. Mable's eyes had already welled with tears and a single drop had streamed down her cheek. She, too, stepped forward and they found themselves in a warm embrace that undeniably spelt the word *forgiveness*.

George soon looked at her and said: "It's not your fault. You are not responsible for any of it, but if you still need to hear these words from me, I willingly utter them: *Mable Ferguson, I forgive you on behalf of my father, Andy, and our entire family*. Release the pain and the guilt now— they don't belong to you."

Speechless and sobbing, Mable held onto George while feeling the weight of the world gradually leaving her shoulders.

~ The End ~

Don't miss the nail-biting sequel in this popular series!

MEET LITTLE ROSIE CULLEN IN
Cornelius' Revenge

"Still get goosebumps just thinking about it." - Amazon customer

"Here we go with the crying again. I loved the fact that we get an older version of the family I fell in love with the first time around. Even sweeter than before and just as heartbreaking at times." - *Amazon customer*

YOUR FREE EXCERPT IS COMING UP NOW!

#1 BEST SELLING AUTHOR
TANYA R. TAYLOR

CORNELIUS'
REVENGE
BOOK 2

THE CORNELIUS SAGA SERIES

1

"Rosie, hurry up! We can't miss our flight," Mira yelled while tying her shoe laces.

"I'm ready now, Mom." Six-year-old Rosie Cullen entered the bedroom moments later. Her pink and white back-pack hung sturdily across a pink, short-sleeved blouse with frilly sleeves. Blue jeans slackly covered her legs and matching pink tennis shoes snuggled her tiny feet. Her black, medium-length candy curls glistened from the extra spiff of her mother's oil sheen. "See, Mom, we look just alike now, except for your blouse— it's blue. I told you pink is fancier."

Mira smiled. "You're probably right, Rosie, but Mom didn't have any pink blouse like yours. Sorry." She stood up. "All set?"

"All set!"

"Perfect! Let's go, then." Mira grabbed the two carry-ons as Rosie led the way to the front door.

Abruptly, the little girl stopped and looked back at her mother. "Is Uncle Wade coming too?"

"I'm afraid not, honey."

"Well, who will I play with at Nana and Pops' house? I'll be so bored. Why can't Uncle Wade send Tommy?" She sulked.

Mira crouched down to her daughter's level. "Your Uncle Wade and Aunt Norma are very busy at the hospital right now. They couldn't break away to fly up the same time as we are and they won't send Tommy on the plane alone."

"So when will we ever see them again? I miss them!" Rosie's big, brown eyes had a tinge of sadness in them.

"I'm sure we'll see them soon. Maybe we'll take a trip down there to The Bahamas one weekend or they can come here to L.A. How'd you like that?" Mira hoped the proposition would excite the child.

"That sounds neat, Mom!" Rosie's mood suddenly elevated. "Okay, let's go." She opened the door and headed outside toward the waiting cab.

Passing the champagne-colored Mitsubishi parked in the driveway in front of their white condominium, Rosie asked: "Why can't we take our own car to the airport, Mom?"

145

"Because I don't want to have to yank my hair out from the hefty fee I'd have to pay when we get back, honey."

"Good morning, Ma'am." The driver was standing next to the cab. He was of slim build; had a prickly beard and dirty-blonde hair tied into a ponytail. Looked like he was well into his fifties.

"Good morning." Mira smiled back, then looked at Rosie.

"Good morning, sir," she said.

"I'll get that for you." The driver quickly opened the back door and Rosie climbed inside.

"Thanks for coming," Mira said to him.

"My pleasure." He took the luggage and placed them in the trunk.

Mira slid inside next to Rosie as the little girl prissily positioned herself onto the leather seat.

"You look beautiful, Mom."

"And so do you, my little princess." Mira tucked back the child's hair.

The cab driver got in and started the engine. He cleared his throat and glanced back at Mira through the rear-view mirror. "All set?" He asked.

Mira's eyes met his. "Yes, we are."

They were on their way.

* * *

"Mom, can I sit by the window?" Rosie asked excitedly.

"Excuse me," a young man said as he brushed past Mira and Rosie who had just arrived at their appointed row.

"Sure honey, you can sit at the window," Mira answered.

Rosie quickly went through and climbed onto the seat. After resting her backpack on top of her lap, she buckled her own seat belt, then eagerly peered out of the window.

"Those men look like ants down there," she remarked.

"No, they don't!" Mira laughed as she fastened her seat-belt. "We haven't lifted off yet. How can they look like ants from this short distance?"

"Well, they do to me!" Rosie returned.

"My goodness… what beautiful hair you have, little girl!" An elderly lady commented as she was slowly passing by.

"Thank you, Ma'am!" Rosie shifted proudly in her seat, pressing her lips together as if she were the queen of that flying castle.

"She seems rather classy too." The lady bent down slightly toward Mira; voice lowered.

"She does. Doesn't she?" Mira grinned.

Smiling, the nice stranger continued on to one of the back rows.

"Can I put that into the overhead compartment for you?" a beautifully-attired attendant asked. She was referring to Rosie's backpack.

"Does she have to take it, Mom?" Rosie pouted.

"You can put it under your seat instead. Would you prefer that?" The lady offered.

"Yes, Ma'am."

"I'll take it for you," Mira reached over and placed it under Rosie's seat as the flight attendant walked off.

Everyone sat quietly as the plane revved for the take-off.

"Ready?" Mira asked Rosie who was looking out the window again. By then, the tarmac was clear.

"Yes, I'm ready. I'm ready to see Nana and Pops again. Are you ready?"

Mira could not recall Rosie's smile being any cuter.

"Yes. We're going to have a great time there. Mom and Dad are so excited to see you again."

"I'm excited to see them too!"

As the plane took off and smoothly elevated into the clear, blue sky, Mira looked over at the ground below.

"Everything down there looks like ants now, don't it?" Rosie turned to her mother.

"Yes, honey."

After a few moments, Mira rested her head on the head-rest. As she shut her eyes, her life in recent years suddenly flashed before her. Before long, she successfully blocked it all out and drifted off into a dreamless sleep.

2

"Mom! Wake up!" Rosie shook her.

Mira peeled open her eyes, looked at Rosie, then around at other passengers who were getting ready to leave the plane. "We're here already?" she asked weakly.

"Mom, you slept the whole while!" Rosie's hand was at her side.

"I...I'm sorry, honey." She raised her eyebrows.

The cabin door opened and persons were filing out of the aircraft. She glanced Rosie's way and realized she already had her backpack on her lap. They both waited until most of the passengers had exited the plane before getting up to join what was left of the line.

"I can't believe we're here already," Mira said quietly as the little girl stood in front of her.

"Time flies. Doesn't it, Mom?"

"It surely does."

With luggage in hand, they followed the others through the long corridor with all its twists and turns, then headed toward the exit. It was a beautiful day in Mizpah and they were so glad to have arrived.

"There's Nana and Pops!" Rosie pointed to her waving grandparents who were standing several feet away from the exit. She took off running toward them and Michael knelt down happily awaiting her. She flew into his arms as Sara hugged her from behind.

It had been several months since Mira last saw her father, but it was obvious that within that time-frame, he had lost a considerable amount of weight. *Must be all that yard work*, she thought.

"So what am I…chopped liver?" she asked, approaching them.

"Oh, honey, I'm so glad you two are here, safe and sound!" Sara embraced her.

Michael stood and hugged Mira as well.

"How are you doing?" he asked.

"Just great, Dad. How are you?"

"Swell! Let me take those." He was referring to the luggage.

Mira released one of the bags and held on to the other. She didn't want him doing much lifting since he had been recently having occasional back pains.

He grabbed the other one as well.

"Dad, I could've managed that," Mira said.

"I'm sure you could, but I can too." He carried them over to the trunk.

"I'm so glad you two are here!" Sara pressed her face against her daughter's.

"We're happy to be here, Mom," Mira replied.

They walked over to the car together.

"How's Dad doing? He seems to have trimmed down quite a bit lately."

"Oh…yes. He's watching his diet more these days. You know him—likes to look his best. I heard from your brother this morning." She changed the subject rather abruptly.

"Oh? What's he saying?"

"He was just wondering if you and Rosie had arrived yet and said he wished he could have come, but he's so tied up at work right now."

"I know. We spoke last night. Rosie really wished Tommy would've been here." She spoke quietly as the little girl stood proudly beside her grandfather at the car filling him in on all the details of their flight.

"Yes, they're so close," Sara returned.

"She'll be fine, though. I'll find things to do to keep her busy during the two weeks we're here."

"*You'll* find things?" Sara asked with a smirk. "What're the rest of us… chopped liver?"

They both started laughing as they got into the car.

* * *

"Here we are..." Sara unlocked the kitchen door and allowed Mira and Rosie to enter first. The family always used that entrance since the carport was right adjacent to it. The front door mostly opened whenever guests showed up.

"It's been several months well; hasn't it?" Sara surmised.

"Yeah." Mira sighed.

"Well, I'm glad you sent Rosie ahead last Christmas since you couldn't make it."

Mira sat down in the living room and Rosie climbed up on the couch next to her.

"She had so much fun with Tommy that visit. Didn't you, pumpkin?" Sara smiled at Rosie.

"I sure did, Nana!"

The proud grandmother grinned. "And you'll have just as much fun this time!"

"Will I?" Rosie was excited only for a moment before her intellect kicked in. "But how? Tommy's not here this time."

"Because Nana and Pops are going to give you the time of your little, young life." She sat across from her. "We're going to play lots of games, go to the park, the movie theater..."

"Movies? Really? We're going to see movies?" Rosie's eyes widened.

"Sure. Why not? Anything our little pumpkin wants to do—that's what we're going to do!"

Rosie got up, ran over to her grandmother and hugged her neck tightly. "Oh, Nana… you're the best Nana in the whole world!"

Sara was smiling from ear to ear as Michael passed with the luggage. "These'll be in your room," he said to Mira.

"Thanks, Dad," Mira replied.

"I almost forgot Dad didn't come in," she mumbled softly.

"He's always been as slow as a turtle, you know." Sara laughed.

"Don't say that about Pops!" Rosie exclaimed.

"Sorry, dear. I'm just joking."

A minute later, Michael joined them and sat in his favorite chair—the one with the invisible *Reserved for Michael Cullen* engraved onto the leather.

"So how's everything up there in California?" He asked.

"Everything's fine, Dad."

"The weather's good?"

"Pretty sunny for the most part," Mira indicated.

As she sat with them, Mira reflected on how quickly time had passed. Her parents now had graying hair—though she felt her mother still looked stunning for her age. She was putting in her last couple of years at the

154

hospital after Michael retired from his executive-level position at the Gaming Board.

Mira remembered the years they had spent in that house—many of them held not-so-good memories, but a few did, particularly the ones after Karlen and Andy's saga came to a close. Her father's almost instant transformation into the man they wished he had been ages before was unforgettable and nothing less than remarkable. Despite his limited communication skills which still remained, by all accounts, he became a wonderful and loving husband and father.

"Still work for that chiropractor?" Michael broke the brief silence.

"He's a cardiologist, Dad, and yes, I'm still there," Mira replied.

Sara was looking on. She could tell that her husband had something he wanted to get off his chest, but wasn't so sure if he should."

Mira noticed too. "Rosie, would you like to watch TV in the bedroom for a while?" she asked.

"Sure. Let's go, Pops!" The child turned to her grandfather.

"Honey, how about you and I go?" Sara proposed.

"You and me, Nana?" Rosie appeared somewhat baffled. "But Pops and I always watch TV together. Aren't you coming, Pops?"

Michael managed a smile. "I'll come in a little while, pumpkin."

"Can we watch *The Twilight Zone*?"

"Sure we can, if it's on."

"I'll see if I can find it, okay?"

"Okay, pumpkin," Michael replied.

Sara and Rosie headed to the master bedroom.

Michael cleared his throat. "So, any thoughts on going back to school and getting your degree?" he asked Mira. "You only had… what… a year and a half left? Something like that?"

"I haven't thought about it lately," Mira answered.

"Why not?" The expression on her father's face was one of concern.

"I just haven't, Dad. A lot's been going on lately like work, getting Rosie into school, and a bunch of other things."

"I see."

Mira interlaced her fingers in her lap. "Dad, I know when you and Mom sent me off to college you guys had big dreams for me… and don't get me wrong, I was the one who gave you the idea that I wanted to become a doctor— just like Wade turned out to be. Instead, I got pregnant, dropped out of school and never went back. And on top of that, I know it seems like I settled for working in a doctor's office instead of becoming one like I had intended, so that's probably another 'slap in the face'. I understand where you're coming from, Dad and I'm really sorry I disappointed you and Mom…"

"You didn't disappoint us, Mira," Michael stated, but then noticed the look of disbelief on her face. "Okay, at first your mother and I felt let-down because we did have high hopes for you, but what I need you to know is that we still believe in you and we don't think any less of you because you got pregnant and dropped out of school. We just hate to see you settle for less than what you always wanted to be; that's all."

"Pops!" Rosie emerged with a grimace. "Nana and I can't find *The Twilight Zone*,"

"Okay, pumpkin. I'll be there in a minute," Michael said.

The little girl quickly headed back to the room.

"Dad, I love my job. Doctor Charles is a wonderful employer and I have lots of benefits there at the clinic," Mira explained. "I'm not saying that I won't eventually go back to school and finish what I started. I'm just waiting for the right time and I really don't think it's now."

"Okay," Michael started to get up. He held his lower back with one hand and leaned on the arm of the chair with the other. "I know you'll do what's best for you and Rosie. It was on my mind for a while, so I thought I'd talk to you about it."

"I understand, Dad."

"I'll go back there now and relieve your mother. She mentioned something about lunch when we were on our way to pick you two up."

Mira watched him slowly make his way to the master bedroom. She was grateful that her father had cultivated such a good relationship with his grandchildren—unlike anything she had ever experienced with him as a child. There was something about him, however, since his recent retirement that made her wonder and even slightly worry about him at times. An inner nudge was telling her that it wasn't because he was simply getting older, but that there was something more to it.

3

"I'm about to make some sandwiches. Wanna help?" Sara was tying her apron in the kitchen.

"Sure, Mom." Mira proceeded over to a side table and grabbed the freshly baked bread sitting on a silver pan.

"When did you bake this?" She started slicing the loaf.

"A few hours ago. It's not so warm anymore, huh?"

"No, but surely smells tasty."

Sara retrieved the cold cuts from the refrigerator.

"Are you sure Dad's okay, Mom?"

"He's doing fine, dear, except for the back pain he whines about occasionally," Sara affirmed.

Mira sat on one of the stools next to the counter and helped her mother make the sandwiches.

"What makes you wonder?" Sara looked at her.

"I don't know. He just seems a little different— mellower I guess."

"Well, that should be expected. Your father's not as young as he used to be. People do tend to get mellower as they age. Don't you think I have?"

"No, Mom. I think not." Mira smirked.

Sara chuckled.

"So any new prospects lately?" Sara kept her eyes on the sandwich she was preparing.

Mira looked at her mother cross-eyed. "What do you mean by *prospects*?"

"You know... you met anyone special yet?"

"Mom, must we always have this conversation? You ask me the same thing at least every three months."

"That's because, you know...you're twenty-eight now, sweet pea and I think it's time that you settled down with someone nice."

"Is this a conspiracy with you and Dad?"

"What do you mean?"

"Dad questioned me about whether I'm going back to school or not and now, in the same hour, you're asking me about my love life."

"There's no conspiracy, dear." Sara's eyes met hers. "But do you have one?"

"What?" Mira scowled. "Do I have what?"

"A love life."

Mira sighed hopelessly.

"Bobby Newton's been asking about you a lot lately."

"For what?"

"He's been a little subtle about it at first," Sara went on, "but I notice that every time you come home to visit, he makes it a point to come see you. He's also been helping your father out in the yard most weekends and helps us with practically anything else we might need."

"Really?" Mira asked.

"Really."

"Why didn't you tell me he was keeping you guys so hot?"

"Well, I'm telling you now." Sara stopped what she was doing and leaned over the counter. "One day, I came right out and asked him."

"Pray tell, what?" Mira was gearing up for the disclosure.

"If he liked you."

"Mom...you didn't!"

"I certainly did!" Sara straightened up again. "It was obvious that he did and I could see that he was just too shy to reveal it."

"What did he say?"

"Do you really want to know?" Sara seemed eager.

Mira thought for a moment and sighed again. "To be honest with you, Mom... No, I don't really wanna know. Bobby's a nice guy and all, but I'm not interested. I just wanna focus on me and Rosie. I don't have any room in my life for a relationship."

Sara's heart sank. "Mira!"

"What?"

"How can you say that? That you don't have any room in your life for a relationship? Don't you want to settle down with someone you can share your life with and grow old together with?"

"I can do that with my daughter, Mom."

"Now, that answer was just plain silly!" Sara's hands were at the waist.

"Not to me."

"For your information, dear, Rosie is going to grow up someday and meet a nice, handsome fella of her own. She's not going to court you, my dear. She'll have her own life to live." She leaned over the counter again. "Look…you've known Bobby ever since grade school and you two have always gotten along so well. Why not give him a chance? He is interested; he straight out told me."

Mira was quiet. Sara could tell that she was analyzing all of the information.

"I'm not interested, Mom," she finally replied.

Sara exhaled heavily. "I can't believe you, Mira!" She was shaking her head. "No man's ever going to be good enough for you. I'm right. Ain't I?"

"I don't know what you're talking about. Why are you making such a big deal of this anyway?" Mira was becoming agitated. "I'm a grown woman now, Mom. If I choose to be by myself for the rest of my life, that's my prerogative. I'm not saying that's what I want. It's just that…"

"No one can ever fit the bill," Sara interjected. "You know what I'm talking about."

"I have no idea, Mom. I really don't."

Sara walked around the counter and sat next to Mira. "Every single fella I knew that showed the slightest interest in you, you push them away."

"You've lost me there."

"Take Rosie's father, for instance. The guy just forgot your birthday and you dumped him!"

"Mother, for your information, Cody and I had been dating for a full two years. There was no excuse for him not to remember my birthday," Mira countered. "Furthermore, it was more than just that."

"Sweet pea, you know that's all it was. Cody was a real gentleman who treated you so well the time you were together. No amount of calls or pleading on his part prompted you to take him back after you broke up with him. I never understood how you could do that."

"You weren't in the relationship with him, Mom. You couldn't see his stupid flaws. Furthermore, if he was such a nice guy and a *gentleman* as you say, how come after he saw that I wasn't getting back with him, he moved away and seemingly forgot he had a daughter. Such a nice guy he is!"

"You're right about that," Sara agreed. "He's so wrong and he'll regret that one day, but let's not make this about Cody...I'm talking about you. Ever since that incident with Karlen Key and Andy all those years ago, you've taken on the viewpoint that love relationships must be perfect—like theirs was."

"I really don't know what you're talking about." Mira looked away momentarily.

"Don't you remember what you said to me that very evening after Karlen and Andy were re-united?"

"No."

"I remember. You said that when you grew up, you would never fall in love with a man if he wasn't like Andy."

"The revelation instantly jogged Mira's memory."

"You said that he was the perfect man and you wanted to have a relationship just like theirs when you grew up," Sara continued.

Mira was silent.

"I think I understand now. You don't think you've found the man that's measured up to the standards you've set based on those qualities you saw in Andy."

"That's ridiculous," Mira finally responded.

"No, it's not and you know I'm right, dear. I realize that experience you had all those years ago - witnessing the extremely passionate, undying love they had for one another made a lasting imprint in your young mind of what love between a couple should be like. But sweetheart, I'm going to be honest with you... Romantic relationships require work. When the butterflies in the stomach settle down, couples tend to come back to reality. The struggles, hardships and disagreements set in and if the love is true and pure from the beginning, it can survive. What you didn't see were the struggles, hardships and disagreements Karlen and Andy might have had with each other when they were courting. You didn't see the attitudes and personalities that clashed from time to time. You just saw the most meaningful part—which is how strong and lasting their love was that even transcended death and that's what was so beautiful and gave you the outlook on life you have today."

"I don't know, Mom. You've arrived at such a deep conclusion to a simple matter," Mira said.

Sara gently stroked her daughter's hair, then got up and walked back around the counter.

"Just think about what I said. I know when you and your brother were younger, you didn't see much affection coming my way from your father and I know that's not what you want for your life. But you know your father is a different man now and these past fifteen years have made up for all the years prior to that. He's more loving, affectionate and although he's still not much of a talker, he communicates way more than he used to. Our love may not be a fairy-tale type of romance, but it's true love and as we're growing old together, we're both grateful that we're here for each other and enjoying life. That's what I want for you—someone you can share your life with in a loving, caring way." She placed two sandwiches on a tray. "I'm going to take these to your father and Rosie."

Mira sat at the kitchen counter, surprised that her mother had even brought up the Karlen and Andy saga.

165

She pulled up one of the sandwiches and took a bite. Her mother was beginning to get inside her head. *Maybe she's right*, she thought. Then in a split second, she decided that she still felt the same way as before and nothing her mother said was going to change that.

That night…

Mira was helping Rosie with her pajama top. The little one had just finished her bubble bath.

"Why do you always do this, Mom? I'm old enough to do it myself," Rosie stated matter-of-factly.

Just then, Sara appeared at the door. "So you're ready for bed now, huh?"

"Yes, Nana," Rosie answered cheerfully. "Umm…Nana, may I watch one more program with Pops before I go to sleep?"

"Now, pumpkin…" Sara stepped further into the room, "…that's completely up to your mother." She glanced at Mira.

"Mom, can I?" Rosie made her plea.

"Honey, it's late. It's actually almost ten o'clock now." Mira glanced at the clock affixed to the wall. "You and Dad have watched television for hours already. Dad has to get some sleep and so do you. There's always tomorrow, okay?"

Sara smiled as she looked on.

"Okay, Mom." Rosie pouted a little as she climbed into bed.

Mira walked toward her mother. "Can they ever get enough of that TV?" Mira remarked. "She's not interested nearly as much when we're home."

"That's because that is their special thing," Sara responded. "Whenever your father passes on..." she lowered her voice to a whisper, "...that's most likely the thing she'll miss the most. They're creating memories that will last a lifetime. Have a good night, dear." She patted Mira's shoulder and left the room.

End of Sample

GET THE FIRST 10 BOOKS IN THE BEST SELLING CORNELIUS SAGA SERIES!

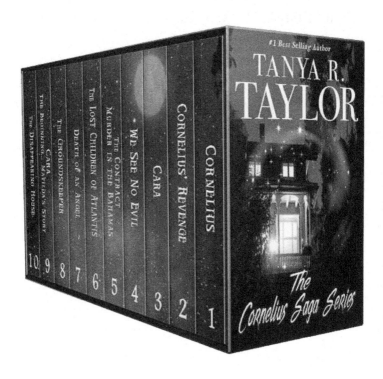

VISIT TANYA-R-TAYLOR.COM

OTHER BOOKS IN THIS BESTSELLING SERIES
(14 as of 2020)

BOOK 2 in the CORNELIUS SAGA

BOOK 4 in the CORNELIUS SAGA

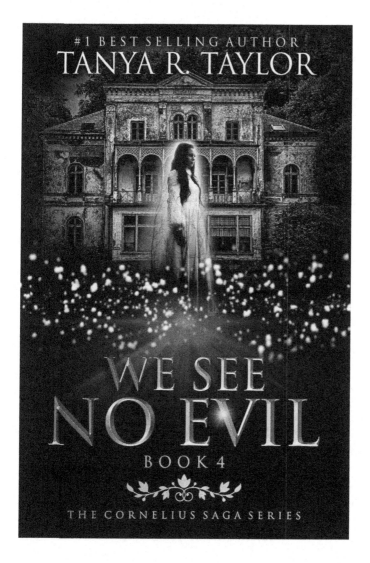

BOOK 5 in the CORNELIUS SAGA

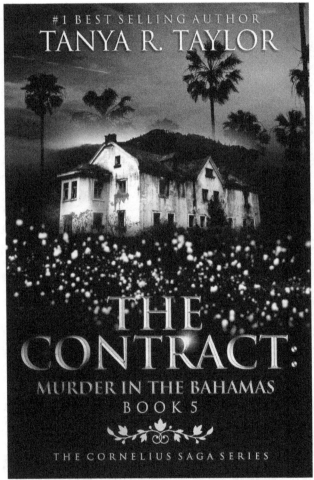

#1 BEST SELLING AUTHOR
TANYA R. TAYLOR

THE
CONTRACT:
MURDER IN THE BAHAMAS
BOOK 5

THE CORNELIUS SAGA SERIES

* Books 1 - 13 in this popular series available at your favorite online bookstore. *

BOOK ONE IN A NEW EXCITING COZY MYSTERY SERIES!

Lucille Pfiffer sees, but not with her eyes. She lives with her beloved dog Vanilla ("Nilla" for short) in a cozy neighborhood that is quite "active" due to what occurred in the distant past. Though completely blind, she plays an integral role in helping to solve pressing and puzzling mysteries, one right after the other, which, without her, might remain unsolved.

The question is: How can she do any of that with such a handicap?

OTHER FICTION TITLES BY THIS AUTHOR
Visit Tanya's website at: tanya-r-taylor.com

INFESTATION: A Small Town Nightmare (The Complete Series)

Real Illusions: The Awakening

Real Illusions II: REBIRTH

Real Illusions III: BONE OF MY BONE

Real Illusions IV: WAR ZONE

Cornelius' Revenge (Book 2 in the Cornelius saga)

CARA: Some Children Keep Terrible Secrets (Book 3 in the Cornelius saga)

We See No Evil (Book 4 in the Cornelius saga)

The Contract: Murder in The Bahamas (Book 5 in the Cornelius saga)

The Lost Children of Atlantis (Book 6 in the Cornelius saga)

Death of an Angel (Book 7 in the Cornelius saga)

The Groundskeeper (Book 8 in the Cornelius saga)

CARA: The Beginning - MATILDA'S STORY (Book 9 in the *Cornelius saga*)

The Disappearing House (Book 10 in the *Cornelius saga*)

Wicked Little Saints (Book 11 in the *Cornelius saga*)

A Faint Whisper (Book 12 in the *Cornelius saga*)

Haunted Cruise: The Shakedown
The Haunting of MERCI HOSPITAL
Hidden Sins Revealed (A Crime Thriller - Nick Myers
Series Book 1)
One Dead Politician (Nick Myers Series Book 2)
10 Minutes before Sleeping

**Get the *heads up* on new book releases
by Tanya R. Taylor.**

**Official Website:
tanya-r-taylor.com**

DON'T MISS OUT ON ANY NEW RELEASES
BY TANYA R. TAYLOR

SIGN UP _NOW_ AT TANYA-R-TAYLOR.COM